Wolfie

Emma Barnes

Emma grew up in Edinburgh, studied at Cambridge and now lives in Leeds. Her first novel, *Jessica Haggerthwaite: Witch Dispatcher*, was shortlisted for the Branford Boase Award and led to her being compared to Roald Dahl and Jacqueline Wilson. She has gone on to write several more books, including the acclaimed *How (Not) To Make Bad Children Good* (Strident Publishing, 2011).

Emma's books have been translated into several languages and broadcast on BBC Radio 4. She regularly visits schools, festivals and libraries, sharing her love of books and reading. If you would like to contact her to discuss a visit please email EmmaJBarnes@yahoo.co.uk or visit her web-site: www.EmmaBarnes.info

Emma Chichester Clark

Emma studied at the Chelsea School of Art and the Royal College, where she was taught by Quentin Blake. Her first book, *Listen To This!*, won the 1988 Mother Goose Award for best newcomer to children's book illustration.

She has illustrated books by Roald Dahl, Kevin Crossley-Holland and Michael Morpurgo, as well as writing and illustrating many of her own books, including *I Love You Blue Kangaroo*, which has won awards in Italy and the USA, and was shortlisted for the Kate Greenaway Medal. *Melrose And Croc Together At Christmas* was a finalist in the Blue Peter Book Awards.

Her most recent books include *Hansel And Gretel*, a collaboration with Michael Morpurgo, and *Alice In Wonderland*, nominated for the 2011 Kate Greenaway Medal.

Wolfie

Emma Barnes

illustrated by Emma Chichester Clark

www.stridentpublishing.co.uk

Published by Strident Publishing Limited, 2012
Text © Emma Barnes, 2012
Cover and interior illustrations © Emma Chichester Clark, 2012

A catalogue record for this book is
available from the British Library.

ISBN 978-1-905537-27-3

Typeset in Gill Sans Light by
Palimpsest Book Production Limited, Falkirk, Stirlingshire
Printed by CPI Group (UK) Ltd

ALBA | CHRUTHACHAIL

The publisher acknowledges support from Creative
Scotland towards the publication of this title.

To Abby . . . and Rocky, her canine friend

CHAPTER ONE
Lucie's Present

"I'm so looking forward to seeing Uncle Joe today," said Lucie on Saturday morning.

"That's nice," said Mum.

"You see, he always brings me a present," Lucie went on.

Mum frowned. "But of course it's Uncle Joe you want to see really."

"No, it isn't, it's the present," Lucie said. "What do you think it will be?"

Mum shook her head at her, and Lucie wondered why grown-ups gave presents at all, if they thought they were such bad things.

"Perhaps he won't bring a present this time," said Mum.

"But he *always* brings a present!"

"You shouldn't think so much about presents," Mum said. Then she smiled suddenly. "But," she added, "I think he *is* bringing a present, and I think it's going to be *even more exciting than usual!*"

Of course, after that, Lucie could think of nothing

else. She was fidgeting about all morning, until Mum said she would read to her in French to calm her down. Mum read her Little Red Riding Hood, which had always been Lucie's favourite, but Lucie kept jumping up and peering out the window.

"Here he is!" she cried when the doorbell rang at last. She ran to open the door. Her parents followed.

Uncle Joe was standing on the doorstep. But he was not alone.

"Hello!" boomed Uncle Joe. "My, Lucie, how you've grown! And hair red as ever, I see!"

Lucie was not listening. She was staring at the animal that stood next to Uncle Joe.

It was BIG — bigger than Lucie.

It had pointed ears and sharp teeth.

It had a silvery coat and sweeping tail.

It had glinting eyes that looked straight at Lucie. They looked as if they wanted to gobble her up.

Lucie raised a shaking hand. "What is *that*?" she whispered, pointing at the creature.

"Oh, that's your present," said Uncle Joe. "A new pet!"

"But what *kind* of pet?"

"Can't you tell? It's a dog, of course!"

Lucie, Mum and Dad stared at the "dog". It stared back at them out of cold, blue eyes. Its long tongue lolled out of the corner of its mouth.

"That's no dog!" said Lucie. "That's a WOLF!"

Anybody could see that, she thought.

The grown-ups laughed. "Don't be silly, Lucie," said Mum.

"Don't be daft, Lucie," said Dad.

"Don't be a juggins, Lucie," said Uncle Joe. "As if I would give you a wolf for a pet!" And the grown-ups laughed so hard Lucie wondered if they would make themselves sick.

"No, it really is a wolf," Lucie said (backing away so the wolf couldn't get her). And she pointed out how big the wolf was, and how sharp its teeth were. And besides, it *looked* like a wolf, not a dog. She even fetched the copy of Little Red Riding Hood so they could look at the pictures.

"*Of course* it's not a wolf," said Uncle Joe chuckling. "The man who sold it to me said it was a dog."

"*Of course* it's not a wolf," agreed Dad. "It's one of those dogs that *look* like a wolf, that's all."

"*Of course* it's not a wolf," said Mum. "It's a German Shepherd, that's what it is."

"It's a wolf," said Lucie.

4

Nobody paid her any attention — except the wolf. It kept watching her out of cold, blue eyes.

They sat down for lunch. Lucie made sure to sit on the opposite side of the table from the wolf. She hoped her parents and Uncle Joe were right. They did know a lot about some things, after all, like computers and vegetarian cooking (Dad) or how to speak French as well as English (Mum) or restoring old motorbikes (Uncle Joe). But Lucie didn't think any of them knew much about animals.

"What are you going to call your new pet, Lucie?" Mum asked.

"I don't know," said Lucie.

"Is it male or female?" Dad asked Uncle Joe.

"Do you know, I didn't ask," said Uncle Joe. "We'd better take a look."

He got up and walked towards the wolf, which was sitting near the kitchen door. A low growling came from the wolf's chest. Like a warning.

"Perhaps another time," said Uncle Joe quickly, sitting down again. "You'll work it out."

"I must say, it's a very *big* dog," said Dad, tucking into onion tart. "I was expecting a puppy."

"They're a lot of hard work, puppies," said Uncle Joe.

5

"It will need a lot of exercise," said Mum. "Still," she added, "We've got a big garden. And there's the park nearby."

Lucie thought about going for a walk in the park — with a wolf.

After lunch Lucie's parents showed Uncle Joe all the things they had done recently to the house, while Lucie wondered what it was grown-ups found so exciting about new bathrooms. Then Dad went to the pet shop and came back with a big sack of vegetarian dog food. They put some in a dog bowl and put it in front of the wolf. The wolf did not seem to like vegetarian dog food.

Dad had bought a dog basket too. But it was much too small for the wolf.

"Funny that," said Dad, scratching his head. "It was the biggest they had. It will just have to sleep on the floor."

After tea, Uncle Joe went home. Then it was time for Lucie's bath. Then bed. Lucie's Dad walked the wolf up and down the street. Then her parents went to bed too.

Lucie lay still in bed, but she did not sleep.

All was dark.

The house grew quieter. And quieter. Eventually it was so quiet you would have been able to hear a pin drop.

Or a wolf, breathing.

CHAPTER TWO
Midnight

The moonlight lay in bars across the floor as Lucie slid her feet from under the covers. Through the gap in the curtains she could see a full moon. The church clock showed midnight.

Gently, ever so gently, she eased open her bedroom door and slipped out onto the landing.

For a moment she stood listening. She could hear nothing at all: no cars on the street, no wind in the leaves. She could not even hear the fridge humming from the kitchen. It was as if the house were under a spell.

Then she heard it again. The gentle pant of a wolf's breathing.

Lucie set off down the stairs. Her feet were bare and made no sound. As she went, she could not help thinking that it was probably not a very sensible thing to do, to go all by herself to see a wolf. But you cannot always be sensible in life. This was something Lucie had already discovered.

She reached the hall, and crossed the cold, red

8

tiles. Slowly, ever so slowly, she pushed open the kitchen door. Then she stepped inside.

The wolf was sitting there, still as a statue, its eyes glittering like marbles in the moonlight.

"Hello, Wolf," whispered Lucie.

For a moment they just watched each other, the red-haired girl in her blue pyjamas, and the great, wild creature, silver in the moonlight.

Then the wolf yawned. Its top lip curled back and its sharp teeth were on display. They were really very sharp indeed.

"Greetings, She-Child," it said.

Lucie felt surprised and not surprised, both at the same time.

"Are you going to eat me?" she asked. It was the first thing that came into her head and she found she very much wanted to know the answer.

"Why do you think I want to eat you?"

"That's what all wolves do. In storybooks, I mean. And you didn't eat any of your dog food."

The wolf looked at her consideringly. "I *could* eat you, I suppose. If it's what you want."

"Oh, it isn't," said Lucie quickly. "Really. What's your name?"

"My name is Fang-That-Bites-Sharp-In-The-Forest,"

9

said the wolf. She curled back her lips, and Lucie saw that her name suited her very well.

"Can I call you Fang for short?" she asked. "Your full name is rather a mouthful."

"Nonsense," said the wolf. "It's not a mouthful. How would *you* like to be shortened?" It glared at Lucie, and she thought it best to change the subject.

"You're a girl wolf, aren't you?" asked Lucie. "A female, I mean."

"Of course. Does that surprise you?"

"Well, it's always a He-Wolf in the storybooks."

"If you think about it," said Fang, "you will realise that it cannot *always* be a He-Wolf. Why they should choose them for the storybooks, I cannot say. There are certainly plenty of us She-Wolves in the world — in so far as there are many of our kind left at all." Suddenly she looked sad.

"But what are you doing in our kitchen?" asked Lucie.

Fang stood up. Lucie was a little alarmed, but it seemed she only wanted to pace back and forth across the kitchen floor. As she did, her shoulders rippled under her great pelt of silvery fur, and her tail swept when she turned, like a great plume feather.

"There are not many places where we wolves are

welcome, She-Child," she said. "Think. Where are the woods and the wild mountains, where the deer run and the wolves can chase them? Where are the caves for the wolves to lodge in the long winter nights? Where are the deep forests, where wolves can gather and howl to the moon?"

"Err, I don't know," said Lucie doubtfully. "There aren't many round here."

"No," agreed the wolf. "There aren't." She sat down next to the dishwasher and began to scratch her hind leg. "So we wolves have to take what we can get." She looked around. "This will have to do."

"It's a lot nicer than our old place," Lucie told her. "Anyway, if you don't like it you could always try a zoo."

A growling sound came from Fang's chest. She turned and looked at Lucie, and her eyes glittered.

"But zoos are horrid," said Lucie quickly. "I'd never want to live in a zoo!"

"My thoughts exactly," said Fang. She looked hard at Lucie. She had very strange eyes. Sometimes they looked blue, at other times grey or green.

Suddenly Lucie felt very solemn.

"Fang," she said, "I'm glad you came to us. I will take care of you. Every way I can. After all, you are meant to be my pet." Even as she said it, she thought how stupid it sounded. A creature like a wolf could never be a pet.

"Very well," said Fang. "*I* will take care of *you* too. Even if you do cut short my name."

"My name's Lucie."

"I know," said Fang. "Ridiculous short names you humans have! But never mind that. Greetings, Lucie. Well met."

Fang bowed her head, and Lucie bowed hers in return. Wolves were obviously very polite animals. Yet there was something wild and untamed about Fang all the same.

Suddenly Fang got up. She went quickly to the back door and sniffed at the bottom of it. Then she stood with her head on one side, listening hard.

"What are you doing?" asked Lucie curiously.

"I thought I heard something," said Fang. "And I am always on my guard. We wolves have our enemies, you know."

Lucie's eyes grew big. "Who?" she whispered.

Fang shrugged, the fur rippling around her broad shoulders. "Humans mainly. They are always trying to lock us up, or kill us. Then there are bad wolves too. Or even The Wolf Catcher. Although I think he is a

story made up to frighten cubs." Lucie shivered, suddenly feeling cold.

"Still," she said quickly, "Mum and Dad always lock the doors and put the burglar alarm on at night. I don't think anybody can get in. Or out."

"Don't be so sure," said Fang. "If I wanted to get out, I would. I have Magical Powers, you know."

"Oh, right," said Lucie. Fang could talk, and that was astonishing enough, but Lucie was not sure she believed in Magical Powers, or not the sort that could magic a wolf through a locked door.

"You wait and see," said Fang, who seemed to guess what she was thinking.

Soon after, Lucie went back to bed. The church clock was chiming one o'clock. Lucie's whole body jumped suddenly, as sometimes happens when you are falling asleep. Her eyes opened and she stared at the ceiling.

Did it really happen? she wondered. *Did I really go downstairs and talk with a wolf? Or was it all a dream?*

But she was too tired to think. And in a few minutes she was fast asleep.

CHAPTER THREE
Breakfast

"Good morning," said Fang as Lucie entered the kitchen next morning.

"Oh good," said Lucie. "You are real, after all."

Fang yawned. "Of course I'm real. Where are your parents?"

"Oh, they always sleep late on Sundays. I hope you were comfortable? The floor is rather hard."

"No matter," said Fang. "A snow-covered forest is no feather bed, I can tell you. It does no good for a wolf to get soft. And now do you think you could find me something to eat? I don't mean to be rude, but that stuff your father gave me is quite inedible!" And she growled, to show just what she thought of the vegetarian dog food.

"I suppose you like meat?"

"I do," said Fang. "Something like a haunch of venison would go down nicely."

"I don't think we have a haunch of venison," said Lucie. "Dad doesn't eat meat. Mum and me do, but we mainly eat things like sausages."

She went to the fridge, and as luck would have it found a pack of sausages on a shelf. "It's a good thing Mum isn't very noticing," said Lucie, fetching a plate.

But Fang did not think much of sausages. They were not what *she* called Fresh Meat, she said, even though Lucie pointed to the date on the packet that showed they were perfectly fresh. She did not see, Fang went on, why human beings had to take perfectly good meat and then chop it up into tiny pieces and stuff it into tubes so that it did not even *look* like meat anymore. "I like something that gives my teeth some exercise," she said. "Something with bone and sinew. Something with *bite*. Wait until I catch you some *real* meat, Lucie."

"Err, actually I *like* sausages," Lucie said. "Do you want these or don't you?"

"No, thank you. We wolves can go for days at a time with no food, you know. I can wait a little longer. Besides, even if your mother is as unnoticing as you say, I don't think we should rouse her suspicions."

"You're probably right," said Lucie, putting the sausages back in the fridge. "Also I think —"

At that moment, the door opened, and Mum came into the room. She was wearing a dressing-gown and still looked half-asleep. "Goodness, Lucie," she said, "who are you talking to?"

"I'm just talking to the wol — I mean Wolfie," said Lucie hastily. "People do talk to their pets you know."

Mum flopped into a chair. "*Wolfie?* You mean the dog? Is that what you've called it?"

She looked at Fang, as if she were noticing her properly for the first time. Fang stared back, looking more wolf-like than ever. Mum fidgeted. "Goodness, it is *big*, isn't it?" she said after a moment.

"Not really," said Lucie. "No bigger than yesterday."

"Well, it looks big to me."

"I like big dogs."

"But they need a lot of exercise."

"Well, we do have the garden — and the park."

"Hmm," said Mum.

"And I'm not sure about the name yet. I might call her Snowy."

Fang gave her a Look which showed just what she thought of Snowy.

"So you've found out it's a she, have you?" said Mum.

"Yes. Err — I could see when I was tickling her tummy."

17

Fang gave Lucie *another* Look.

Mum sighed. "I don't know, Lucie. I have to say I'm wondering now why Uncle Joe didn't give us something a bit smaller —"

"But you hate little yappy dogs!" said Lucie quickly.

"It wouldn't have to be *little*. Just about any dog would be smaller than — than Wolfie."

"But I like her!"

"And Wolfie might be better off living with someone else, someone who could take her for long walks, maybe someone who lived in the country."

Lucie thought about Fang living in the country. She imagined Fang in a field of nice, plump sheep. But in any case, there was no way she was ever giving up her wolf.

"No!"

"We could get a poodle. We could call it Fifi or Minette —"

"NO!" yelled Lucie. "She's mine!"

"But yesterday you kept saying she was a wolf."

"I know," said Lucie. She made herself laugh. "What a silly! As if Uncle Joe would ever give me a wolf! Hee hee!"

She kept laughing in this silly way, until Mum joined in and laughed in a silly way too. After that Mum made herself some coffee and managed to drink it without glancing all the time at Fang — or not more than once every two minutes. But when they heard Dad's feet coming down the stairs, Mum nipped out of the kitchen and went to meet him in the hall.

Lucie sneaked over to the kitchen door. It was open just a crack and she put her ear right against the gap. She could hear Mum rattling on, and the words "un chien énorme!" and then Dad said, "You know I never understand a word you say when you rattle on in French."

After that they whispered in English. Lucie could only catch the odd phrase.

"...seems to have her heart set on it...know what I think...*far* too big...what will it *eat*...doesn't like that dog food...way it stares at you...quite peculiar."

"Nonsense, Louise," said Dad in a much louder voice. "You didn't feel like this yesterday. *I* think it's a fine animal. And it will make a splendid guard dog."

"I suppose so." Mum sounded doubtful.

"Anyway, it was a present."

"True...and she likes it now. Oh dear. Well. We'll have to keep an eye on things, that's all."

Lucie scooted away from the door. Fang gave her another Look, as if to say she didn't think much of eavesdropping. "It's all very well looking down your nose," Lucie hissed. "But it's about *you*, you know."

She sat down quickly and was eating her cornflakes when her parents came into the room.

"Well, well, here you are with your new pet," said Dad heartily, as if he hadn't just been talking about them in the hall. "Sleep well? I must say it was very good in the night. I didn't hear a bark or a whine."

Fang looked down her nose.

"I think she's very polite," said Lucie.

"*Polite?*" said Dad,

"Well-trained, I mean."

"Oh. Right. Well, that's good — isn't it Louise?" Dad went to pour himself some coffee. "Eaten any of its food yet?"

"I don't think she likes it."

"She'll get used to it. Or we could buy her some tinned stuff. Doggy Chunks they call it — you know the kind of thing. What do you think?"

Lucie thought that a Wolf who turned up her nose at sausages was not likely to think much of Doggy Chunks. "We could try," she said doubtfully. "Or — how about a haunch of venison?"

For some reason her parents thought this very funny. "The things you come up with!" said Dad.

"Don't worry. I don't think her taste will be as refined as that."

Fang snorted.

"What's that?" asked Dad, surprised.

"She sneezed," said Lucie hurriedly. "That's all."

She could see that it was going to be tricky at times, having a wolf for a pet.

CHAPTER FOUR
Just Right For Elevenses

After breakfast, Lucie showed Fang the house and the back garden. In the garden they felt safer, knowing that Lucie's parents couldn't hear them. "Still," Lucie said to Fang, "we must be careful not to speak too loud. There are the neighbours, after all."

"What neighbours?" asked Fang.

Lucie pointed. "On that side there's an old professor. I don't think he goes out much. I've never seen him in all the time we've lived here." Fang looked where Lucie was pointing, to the far side of a high wall where a twisted turret stuck out of some thick holly trees.

"He doesn't sound much of a worry."

"No," Lucie agreed, "but on the other side are the Mainwarings, and they're horrible."

Fang looked at the high wall that separated Lucie's garden from the Mainwarings. Then she sniffed.

"They certainly don't smell nice. I detect all kinds of nasty chemicals — plastic and washing detergent —" ("That will be Mrs Mainwaring," said Lucie, impressed) "and then sort of bad cheese and vinegar —" ("I bet that's Marcus!" said Lucie) "but wait a minute! What's this? Something a lot more interesting..."

Fang went very still. Her ears flattened close to her head, then pricked up sharply. She sniffed again. Then she pressed her body low to the ground — and the next moment sprang high onto the garden wall.

As Lucie stared, Fang disappeared into the Mainwarings' garden. Lucie was too astonished to call out.

A moment later Fang reappeared on top of the wall. Then she dropped down beside Lucie. She was carrying something in her mouth.

"What have you got there?" asked Lucie. Fang dropped it on the ground at Lucie's feet. With a sick feeling, Lucie saw it was a rabbit. For a moment she hoped it might be a toy rabbit. Or a model rabbit. That would explain why it was lying so very still. But it was a real rabbit with brown fur and floppy ears. And Lucie recognised it. Before Fang had grabbed it, it had been Marcus Mainwaring's pet. Now — well, it wasn't looking too healthy.

Fang licked her lips. "This is more like it," she said. "Fresh, juicy rabbit. Just right for elevenses."

"You're not going to eat it!"

"Of course I am," said Fang. "It's lovely and plump. You can try a bit if you like."

"I *don't* like!"

"Suit yourself," said Fang. She licked her lips.

"That rabbit is Marcus's pet," Lucie said. "What will he say if you eat it?"

Fang shrugged. "Who cares? I thought you said Marcus was horrible, anyway?"

"He *is* horrible. But you can't go round eating peoples' pets. It's — it's not polite." She thought this point might appeal to Fang, who was an extremely polite wolf.

"How silly," said Fang coldly. "All this fuss about a rabbit. *It's* not clever. *It* can't talk."

"Maybe not," said Lucie. "But you still shouldn't have killed it!" There were tears in her eyes. She thought about the poor rabbit, innocently sitting in its run. The next moment, Fang had nabbed it. It really didn't bear thinking about.

There was a brief silence.

"Actually, it isn't dead," said Fang sulkily. "I think it's just stunned." She prodded the rabbit with her paw, and it sat up, trembling.

"Thank goodness for that!" said Lucie. She picked

up the rabbit and hugged it to her chest — just in case Fang should eat it after all. "*Now* what shall we do?"

Fang looked bored. "I suppose if you *really* don't want me to eat it, I could take it back."

Lucie pictured Mrs Mainwaring looking out of her kitchen window to see a wolf bounding across the lawn. "No! I'll take it round the front."

So while Fang waited in Lucie's garden, Lucie went round to the front of the house and rang the Mainwarings' doorbell.

CHAPTER FIVE
Marcus Mainwaring

Lucie had hoped Mrs Mainwaring would answer, even though she didn't like her much. But Marcus answered — which was far worse.

Marcus and Lucie were exactly the same age. They lived next door. They were in the same class at school. Their parents were always saying things like, "Isn't it *nice* to have another child living next door" and "why don't you go round and make friends?" But of course only parents thought that just because you were the same age, and lived next door, and went to the same school, you had to be friends. Marcus and Lucie didn't think so — in fact, it was one of the few things they both agreed on.

"What're you doing with Gnasher?" Marcus snarled. And he grabbed his pet.

"Gnasher!" said Lucie. "That's a funny name for a rabbit! What does he gnash — apart from carrots?"

"He's fiercer than he looks!" Marcus told her.

"He *looks* about as fierce as a lettuce."

Marcus scowled. He had never liked Lucie, right

from the start. And how dare a sissy girl like her make fun of Gnasher! "What are you doing with him, anyway?" he demanded.

"He was in my garden," said Lucie. (Well, this was *sort* of true.) "So I brought him back. You'd better make sure he can't get out of his run in future." (And then, she thought, maybe Fang won't get *in* either.)

"He *can't* get out," said Marcus, scowling. "Not by himself. You stole him."

"Don't be silly. If I'd stolen him, then why would I bring him back?"

"Because you knew I'd find out!"

Lucie shrugged. She could see that Marcus was determined to pick a fight, whatever she said. He was that kind of person.

"You're just jealous because you haven't got a pet!" Marcus said.

"No I'm not! And I have got a pet! I've got my own wol— dog!"

"What's a wool-dog?"

"Dog!" Lucie shouted. "Dog! Dog! Dog!"

"All right, so they've bought you a dog," said Marcus sourly. "So what? Who wants a dog? And I bet it's a silly, fluffy, yappy dog, with a pompom tail —"

"No, it's not," said Lucie indignantly. "*My* dog —"

But Marcus wasn't listening. He was staring at something, and his mouth had dropped open and his eyes goggled, so that he looked like a goldfish.

Fang was coming up the garden path. She looked beautiful and big and ferocious.

"See? I told you," Lucie said.

Marcus raised a shaking hand and pointed at Fang. "Wh– what kind of dog is it?"

"I'm not sure," said Lucie, as Fang arrived and stood next to her. "But she's ever so fierce when she wants to be."

Marcus's face screwed up tight into its meanest look. He said: "You've no business having a dog like that, Lucie Firkettle. No business at all! And there's something very fishy about this! Very fishy indeed. And I'm going to find out what it is!"

And he went inside, shutting the door with a bang.

"Oh dear," said Lucie.

"You were right," said Fang. "Nasty little beast. Reminds me of a polecat I once knew. I sent *him* scuttling down his hole I can tell you!"

"Ssshh!" said Lucie. "I wish he hadn't seen you."

They walked back to Lucie's garden.

"A polecat — or maybe a weasel," Fang mused to herself. "Anyway, he was bound to see me sooner or later. He only lives next door."

"I know," said Lucie. "But he's a mean one. He'll make trouble if he can."

"I could sort him out," said Fang, snapping her jaws.

"No," said Lucie firmly.

"No what?"

"You're *not* to eat Marcus! However horrible he is!"

Fang looked disappointed. "Oh, all right," she said. "Anyway, I don't think he would taste good."

Lucie was relieved to hear that. But she had a feeling she had not heard the last from Marcus.

CHAPTER SIX
"That's Not a Wolf!"

Fang settled in surprisingly quickly. Mum said nothing more about Fang (or Wolfie, as she called her) being too big. In fact, she and Dad seemed glad that Lucie had a companion. Although both Mum and Dad were around the house a lot during the day, in another way they weren't around, because they were always working. Dad was usually hunched over his computer, writing computer programmes, and Mum taught French to people who came to the house, so neither of them had much time for Lucie. They were glad Lucie had Wolfie, especially as it was still the summer holidays.

Marcus's Mum, on the other hand, worked out of the house. This meant that Marcus spent a lot of time in summer camps, which suited Lucie and Fang just fine. They hardly ever saw him.

Lucie loved being with Fang. She was so clever. She could smell things before she saw them, and hear things that were happening on the other side of the house. She showed Lucie stuff she had never noticed before, even on Acorn Avenue, like a foxes' den, or hedgehogs, or a blackbirds' nest. And she could run like the wind. Every night Fang slept next to Lucie's bed. In the middle of the night, jolted awake by a bad dream, Lucie would hear Fang's steady breathing, and feel safe again.

Best of all, there was a big park near Lucie's house, and as long as she went with Fang, her parents let her go without them. Their favourite part (although Lucie's parents did not know this) was the wild bit on the far side where there weren't many people and there were woods and a gorge with a stream. Fang could run about and get some real exercise. She showed Lucie how to spot kingfishers. She also caught fish and rabbits to eat.

Lucie did not mind about the fish, but she *did* mind about the rabbits.

"Do you *have* to eat them?" she asked, looking the other way while Fang gnawed on a hind quarter.

Fang licked her lips. "Yes," she said simply. "I must eat meat. Or would you rather I ate little girls?"

Lucie jumped.

"Just my little joke," said Fang. "I wouldn't really eat little girls." She winked. "Too chewy."

"Humph," said Lucie. Of course Fang *was* a wolf, and a wolf could not live off bread and butter. But sometimes Lucie wished she could just go to a supermarket and buy a big tin marked Wolf Food — as Sophie had done in the story after the Tiger Came for Tea.

"*You* eat meat," Fang pointed out. "You eat cows and pigs and chickens."

"I know. But they are kept on farms."

"Exactly," said Fang. "Poor things. At least these rabbits have a good time right up until I eat them."

Lucie had to admit that this was true.

Afterwards they walked down to the lake. Lucie often brought bread for the ducks, and enjoyed feeding them; and Fang enjoyed snapping playfully at the gulls if they came too close (at least, Lucie *hoped* she was being playful). But today she had forgotten the bread, and because it was such a nice day and she did not want to go home, she wandered into the children's playground.

It was a very sunny day, and lots of parents had brought their children to play on the swings and slides. Lucie made her way towards the swings, with Fang beside her. Some of the grown-ups were sitting on benches, chatting. Some of them looked up as Fang passed. But none of them said anything. They just turned back to their conversations.

Then a little boy looked straight at Fang. He stood staring at her for a long time. Then he lifted a hand, pointed, and shouted, "Wolf!"

Everything went still. The children stopped playing. The parents stopped gossiping. Everybody turned and stared at Fang, who suddenly looked very big and very...*wolf-like*.

Lucie knew she had to do something quickly. She reckoned she only had a moment before everyone started screaming.

"*Of course* she's not a wolf," she said as loudly as possible. "I mean, how *could* she be a wolf? What an idea!"

Still nobody said a word. Lucie remembered talking to Mum in the kitchen. She forced a laugh. "I mean — a wolf! Ha, ha! Hee, hee!" She kept going. "Ho ho! Tee hee!"

It wasn't working. They were still staring at Fang.

"Fang!" Lucie whispered. "Roll on your back!"

But Fang just gave her a Look that said that she wasn't going to roll about on her back, like a silly dog, for anything.

So Lucie tried one last time. "I mean — just think of it! *Whoever heard of a* WOLF *in a children's playground!*" She forced herself to giggle.

Slowly the terrified faces relaxed. They began to grin. Then they began to laugh. "Ha ha ha! A wolf in a children's playground? How ridiculous!" A few wiped tears from their eyes.

And the next moment everybody had gone right back to their gossiping, their swinging, their sliding or cheerful shrieking. It was just as if nothing had ever happened.

Except for the small boy who had shouted in the first place. He stared at Fang solemnly with his thumb in his mouth.

"Don't worry," Lucie whispered. "She's a *nice* wolf."

The boy nodded and toddled off to the roundabout.

"It really was strange," said Lucie to Fang later. "You'd think everybody would have run away. After all, there you were, teeth and everything. Running away would have been the sensible thing to do."

"Agreed," said Fang. "How you humans get by I can't imagine. Rabbits now — they would have been off like the wind. And rabbits have no brain at all. But you humans seem even stupider than rabbits. How you've done so well as a species is beyond me."

"I think," said Lucie slowly, "because they didn't

expect a wolf to be there, they decided that there wasn't a wolf after all."

"That's it," Fang agreed. "They didn't believe their eyes and nose. Not that you humans have much of a nose. Now rabbits —"

"Or was it your Magic Powers?" Lucie interrupted. "Maybe they protected you?"

"No," said Fang cheerfully. "It wasn't magic. It was just what you said. They decided they couldn't have seen something, so they didn't."

"Well," said Lucie, "at least it means we can go to the playground whenever we want."

So they did, and to lots of other places too. If people ever looked at Fang strangely, and even muttered the word "wolf", then Lucie knew what to do: "Whoever heard of a wolf in a garden centre!" or "Whoever heard of a wolf in a skate park!" or "Whoever heard of a wolf on a bus!" and then laugh as hard as she could. It always worked.

So the days went by until one Sunday Lucie was quieter than usual. She grew quieter and quieter, until by evening she hardly said anything at all.

Fang noticed. "What's the matter with you?" she asked just before bedtime.

"Oh, nothing."

"There must be something. You look like a bear that's woken up only to find it's still winter."

Lucie sighed. "It's the opposite really. I keep hoping and hoping it's still summer, but today is the last day of the school holidays.

"Tomorrow I go to school."

CHAPTER SEVEN
School

"Why are you wearing those terrible clothes?" asked Fang the next morning, as instead of her usual jeans and T-shirt Lucie pulled on a grey skirt and white polo shirt.

"They're my school clothes," said Lucie gloomily. "Look at these horrible shoes! And this! This is the worst of all!"

She waved a red sweatshirt at Fang. It was a very peculiar red. Exactly the shade of red, in fact, to clash most horribly with Lucie's gingery hair.

"Don't you hate this red?" demanded Lucie. "It looks like raw meat!"

"What's wrong with raw meat?" asked Fang. "I find raw meat attractive."

"Only because you can't see the colour," said Lucie.

They had already discovered that Fang could not see colours in the way that Lucie did. Fang said this was only fair. After all, Lucie could not smell or hear half the things that Fang could, and in some ways her eyesight was worse too. "At dusk and dawn," Fang remarked, "or in a dark and shady wood, you see barely half the things that *I* do. I would hesitate to take you hunting by moonlight, for fear that your poor sight would get you into trouble. So it is only fair that you can see these "colours" where I cannot."

Now Lucie sighed. "Well, I wish I couldn't see this red sweatshirt, and I wish nobody else could either!"

Downstairs Lucie's parents were eating breakfast. Lucie tried to force down some cornflakes but she was not hungry.

"Lucie!" said Mum suddenly. "You look different."

"Of course," said Dad. "It's school today. I expect you are looking forward to seeing all your friends!"

They beamed at her. Lucie mashed her cornflakes with a spoon.

"*Why* do I have to go to school?"

They stared at her, astonished.

"To see your friends," said Dad.

"To learn things," said Mum.

"I don't have any friends," Lucie muttered, "and I could learn at home from a book."

Her parents looked at each other.

"But *everybody* goes to school!" said Mum. "So you must too."

They both nodded, as if they had proved something. But really, as Lucie said to Fang later, in the garden, they had proved nothing. Why *should* Lucie go to school, just because everybody else did? Why should anybody do anything, just because everybody else did? What if they were doing something silly, or cruel? What if they were —

"Shooting wolves and chopping down forests," suggested Fang.

"Exactly."

"Or putting wolves in zoos."

"Yes."

"Or keeping rabbits in hutches, instead of doing the sensible thing, and eating them."

"Well..." said Lucie.

"Still, we wolves can be a bit the same," said Fang surprisingly. "All pack animals can. They like to be the same as the rest of the pack. But remember, the best kind of wolf can fend for itself, outside the pack, when it needs to. You and I are not *just* pack animals, Lucie. We think for ourselves."

Lucie nodded. And suddenly she felt a lot better.

Because it was the first day of term, Mum took Lucie to school by car. Fang sat on the back seat beside her.

Lucie gazed through the window at the swarms of children, in their raw-meat-coloured sweatshirts, and felt sick. Fang licked her lips.

"Bye-bye coco," said Mum, pulling in at the kerb.

Lucie hugged Fang and got out of the car. She watched as it pulled away.

Why did other people like school, she wondered? Of course it did not help that she had been new last term, when her family had moved into town. Everyone else had friends already, and Lucie always seemed to be on her own. And it was more than that. *I'm not a school sort of person*, she thought. Then she wondered if they would make fun of her red hair, the way they had last term.

She had told Fang about that last night. "If *I* were to come with you into school," said Fang, "these ill-mannered children might think again." And she snapped at the air, just as she snapped at the gulls by the lake. Lucie had smiled. "Thank you, Fang. I'm afraid children are not as polite as wolves. They don't care about people's feelings."

Now Lucie lifted her chin firmly. *You are not* just *a pack animal*, she reminded herself. *You can fend for yourself.* She marched through the school gates.

Her bold mood lasted until halfway across the

playground. Then she saw Marcus Mainwaring, with his friends Toby and Abdullah.

"Hello Carrots," said Marcus.

Hello Turnip Face, thought Lucie — but she didn't say it aloud.

From the grin on his face, Marcus had been looking forward to tormenting Lucie.

"In that top you look like a blood orange," he told her. "Red and orange mixed together. Yuk!"

"Or ketchup mixed with mustard," suggested Toby. They all snickered.

Lucie blushed. Her top and hair *did* look horrible together. She knew they did.

Some more kids drifted over: Marcus repeated his little joke and they giggled.

"I've thought of a whole lot of new names for you," Marcus went on. "Today it's Blood Orange. Tuesday, Ginger Nut. Wednesday, Tangerine Dream. Thursday, Traffic Lights. Friday —"

"Hey! New girl — what's your name?" A bigger boy wandered over to join the group. Everybody recognised him, even Lucie who had never spoken to him: Alex Beamer from the year above. He played the saxophone, was the best in the school at art, and was the star of the school football team.

"Today she's called Blood Orange," Marcus told him. "You can shorten it if you like to —"

"Who asked *you*?" said Alex, his brows coming down in a way that made him suddenly forbidding. "Anyway, what's with the stupid names?"

"It's because of my red hair," said Lucie.

"What's wrong with red hair?" demanded Alex. There was a pause. Everybody realised what they should have done before — that Alex had red hair too. His was more coppery than Lucie's, but both were red.

"Err —" said Marcus.

"Go away," said Alex.

Marcus opened his mouth and shut it again. Then he slouched off, as if that was what he meant to do anyway. The others drifted after him.

"There's some real oafs in your year," said Alex, watching Marcus go. "You tell me if you have any more trouble. What *is* your name, anyway?"

"Lucie Firkettle."

"I'm Alex." He looked at her almost shyly. "You're the girl with the dog, aren't you? The fantastic, amazing dog! I saw you in the park one time. Wow! I wish I had a dog like that."

Lucie beamed and the next thing they were

chattering away about Fang as if they had known each other all their lives. Alex thought Fang — though they both called her "Wolfie" — was almost as wonderful as Lucie did. "My sister does too. She's only tiny. She thought Wolfie really was a wolf!"

Lucie was so pleased with Alex that on impulse she decided to confide part of her secret to him. "D'you know," she whispered. "There really *is* wolf blood in her."

"Wow!" said Alex. "Amazing! That would explain why I couldn't find one like her in the dog books. Even the ones that live in the north, and pull sleds and herd reindeer. She's fantastic, anyway. I wish *I* had a dog!"

But Lucie had just had a nasty shock. Marcus was loitering close by — much nearer than she'd thought. She hoped that he had not heard what she'd told Alex...but she had a horrible feeling that he had.

CHAPTER EIGHT
Marcus the Spy

When Lucie came skipping out of the school gates at going-home time, Fang was waiting for her.

"Hello," Lucie said. She rubbed behind Fang's ears, the way she especially liked, and Fang made a growly noise which meant she was happy.

"So how was school?" Fang asked, once there was nobody to overhear.

"Actually better than I expected. Marcus was his usual pig self, of course. But then this big boy, Alex, sorted him out. He's really nice — I think we might even be friends! He really likes *you*, Fang — he's going to come round and meet you one afternoon when he doesn't have football practice. And he told me about Art Club at lunch time, in Mrs Donnegan's classroom, so it doesn't matter that nobody plays with me — I mean to say, I'd rather do art — and I'm doing a wonderful picture of a wolf and my teacher says I can work on it in class too —"

Lucie stopped. Fang had her nose in the air and a displeased expression on her face. "Well, I'm glad you've had such a good time," said the wolf. "I would hate to think you were pining. Or that you had missed me. Of course, it wasn't much fun for *me* all day, sitting at home by myself."

"But of course I'd rather be with you! Just because school wasn't as horrible as I expected...you're still my best friend!"

"Oh. So you did miss me a little bit..."

"I missed you A LOT! And I don't want you to be lonely either!"

"Oh, don't worry about that." Fang looked more cheerful. "A wolf can always do with a little quiet thinking time."

They turned into Acorn Avenue and saw Mum hurrying towards them. She had her jacket on inside-out, and odd shoes, and her hair was all on end.

"Oh Lucie!" she cried, hugging her. "I only just realised the time! Mr Fosdyke was here for his lesson, and I was trying to explain to him the subjunctive — but alors! — he is vraiment stupide!"

"Don't worry, Mum," said Lucie. "Wolfie came to collect me."

Mum hugged Fang too. Fang rolled her eyes.

"What a wonderful dog! And how was school, my pet?"

"Actually — it was OK," said Lucie.

"There you are!" cried Mum, very pleased with herself. "See, parents always know best!"

It was Lucie's turn to roll her eyes.

* * *

After that, Fang always collected Lucie from school. The big wolf looked very strange sitting on the pavement amongst all the gossiping parents and the babies in prams. However, nobody paid much attention, except for Alex, who would come over to say hello, sometimes with his little sister Grace. Grace loved Fang too and often brought a treat that she had saved from her own meal. Fang always made a great show of gobbling them up, even if she did not like them.

"Sweaty cheese and bacon rind are *not* what wolves like best to eat," she would say to Lucie afterwards. "But she's only a little cub and she means well."

Lucie's parents never seemed to wonder about the way that Fang came and went by herself. Sometimes Lucie thought her parents were not very bright or very noticing. After all, even the biggest, most intelligent dog does not go in and out of a shut door by itself — especially a *locked* door.

"How *do* you get in and out?" Lucie asked Fang.

They were sitting in the back garden. Lucie was piling conkers on the path, and Fang was spread out next to her.

Fang yawned.

"Well, how do you?" asked Lucie again, rather surprised that Fang had not replied.

Fang still said nothing. But she sniffed, as if to say "can't you smell something?" and flicked her ears as if to say "and hear something too?"

And Lucie *did* hear something — a rustle of leaves. She looked up.

A chestnut tree grew close to the garden wall. Where its leaves hung thickest, there suddenly appeared a *face*. It gave Lucie a shock. For one thing, it had such a mean look. For another, it belonged to her least favourite person in the whole world — Marcus Mainwaring.

"I hate to break it to you, Lucie," sneered Marcus, "but she doesn't *talk* you know! There's a reason they're called *dumb* animals!" He leaned a bit further forward. "But don't worry — you go on playing your little imaginary games if you want to!"

He pulled himself onto the very top of the wall, and stood there, smirking.

"You mean pig, Marcus!" shouted Lucie. "Spying and sneaking!"

Marcus grinned. But he was not concentrating and lost his balance. He began flailing with his arms, like a windmill. He wobbled forward...he wobbled backwards... he tried to grab hold of the branch of the chestnut tree. He *almost* got hold of it...*almost*...but not quite...

"Help!" He lost his grip and went slithering down the other side of the wall. THUMP!

"Serve you right!" Lucie shouted.

There were rustlings and mutterings as Marcus picked himself up. These grew fainter as he made his way back to his own house. Then there was a distant BANG! as he slammed the back door.

Lucie waited a moment. "What a creep!" she said to Fang at last. "Spying on us!"

"Definitely more of a weasel than a polecat," Fang replied.

* * *

But Lucie had just made a big mistake. She thought that Marcus had gone indoors. He had not.

On his way back to the house, feeling very sorry for himself, with his hands and knees stinging where he had grazed them in his fall, Marcus had suddenly had an idea. His idea was *not* to creep back and spy on Lucie and Fang again, now that they were off their guard. Oh no. It was a lot more petty than that. He decided to take them by surprise and throw things at them.

So he slammed the back door — but from the outside. Then, tiptoeing so they would not hear him, he went to gather twigs and moss from the base of the tree. He found some nice, prickly horse chestnut cases too. He shoved them into his pockets and was just about to start climbing when he heard Lucie speak.

"What a creep! Spying on us."

"Definitely more of a weasel than a polecat."

Marcus almost jumped out of his skin. Who had said *that*? It wasn't Lucie and it didn't sound like Lucie's Mum or Dad either. In fact, it was like no voice that Marcus knew. It couldn't...no, it couldn't possibly be...

"We'll have to be careful though, Fang," said Lucie after a while.

"We certainly will. Nasty little beast. I've *still* got

the smell of him in my nostrils. Urgh! It does hang about. Come on, Lucie. Let's go."

Marcus waited a few moments, then swung himself into the tree. Cautiously, he peered over the top of the wall.

Lucie and Fang had their backs to him as they walked towards the house. There was nobody else there at all.

Marcus sniggered to himself as he watched them disappear inside.

"You just made a big mistake, Lucie Firkettle," he said aloud. "You and that ugly brute of yours. The biggest mistake of your life."

CHAPTER NINE
Marcus Plots

"Why can't *I* have a dog?" Marcus asked his mother next morning as they sat eating breakfast in their immaculate kitchen.

"Horrid, smelly, messy creatures," said Mrs Mainwaring at once. "Pooing everywhere. Shedding fur. I hate them. Almost as much as I hate children," she added.

Marcus did not take that personally. His mother ran a nursery.

"Noisy too," went on Mrs Mainwaring. "Barking and yapping. That one next door doesn't bark, thank goodness. But it was howling the other night. Looked out of the window and there it was, howling in the moonlight. Gave me quite a shock, I can tell you." She scowled, remembering. "Looked almost like — almost like a *wolf*."

"Maybe it *is* a wolf," said Marcus.

"Don't be stupid," snapped Mrs Mainwaring. "Whoever heard of a pet wolf?" She got up and went to wash up her breakfast things.

"It could be," Marcus said. "That Lucie has a book about wolves at school. I took it — I mean, I borrowed it — when she wasn't looking. And that dog looks just like the pictures. Maybe it really IS a wolf."

"And maybe pigs can fly," said Mrs Mainwaring.

"What would happen if it *was* a wolf?"

"They'd stick it in a zoo," said Mrs Mainwaring at once. "Or shoot it. But it's not a wolf." She put on her rubber gloves and began spraying disinfectant all over the counters. "I'm certainly going to complain if I hear it howling again," she added.

"I still don't see why that Lucie should have a dog and not me," whined Marcus.

"You've got a rabbit, haven't you?"

"Only because the nursery rabbit had babies. *I* never wanted a rabbit."

"Then give it to next door's dog," said Mrs Mainwaring nastily. "I'm sure it would take care of it for you. Now get moving, Marcus, I'm late."

She hurried out of the sparkling kitchen to find her coat. Marcus was still thinking over their conversation. Certain phrases kept niggling at him: *stick it in a zoo* and *shoot it* and *give it to next door's dog*. He realised he was getting an idea.

A mean, cruel, cunning idea. Just the kind he liked best.

"What if it was a *talking* wolf?" he said to his Mum as they left the house. "What then?"

"Be your age! There are no talking wolves!"

"But if there were?"

"Interview it on the telly, I expect," said his mother sarcastically. "Ask it what it thinks of the world economic situation. Really, Marcus, how should I know? I suppose they'd lock it up in a laboratory, and do tests on it. What stupid ideas you have! Talking wolves! It'll be fairies and hob-goblins next."

She went clicking away up the pavement on her high heels. Marcus grinned to himself. "Just shows what you know," he said.

* * *

Next door, Lucie was still eating her breakfast. Naturally, she had no idea that Marcus was plotting. Instead, she was thinking about the picture she was going to do at school, and how she and Fang were planning to go looking for more conkers together afterwards.

She hummed to herself as she spooned up her cornflakes. Her parents were both listening to the news on the radio, but Lucie did not pay much attention until Dad suddenly choked on his tea.

"Well, what do you know," he said, when he'd stopped spluttering. "That's old Professor Pike they're talking about — Professor Pike who lives next door!"

"Do you really think it's the same one?" asked Mum.

"Must be!" said Dad. "Hush!"

They all listened hard, even Lucie, but they had missed most of it. "....awarded for distinguished contributions to scientific research," said the announcer. "And now, moving on to the sports results..."

"Must be a brainy old bird," said Dad.

"Are you sure it's the *same* Professor Pike?" asked Mum.

"But what was it *about*?" asked Lucie.

"They just said our Professor Pike has been awarded a Gold Medal," Dad said. "For distinguished scientific research. I think it's the same one. Rather good to think we live next door to a Gold Medal Winner. Wish they'd said what kind of scientific research it was — wonder if it had anything to do with computers —" Dad finished munching his toast and slipped the crust to Fang, who crunched it whole.

"I wish you wouldn't feed Wolfie at table," said Mum. She gazed at Fang. "I must say she is looking very well. Wonderful, glossy coat she has."

"It's that vegetarian dog food," Dad said. "Full of vitamins."

As she left for school with Fang, Lucie found herself gazing at the house next door with new curiosity. It was a very odd-looking house. It had a high wrought-iron gate with gateposts with gargoyles on top, and it was surrounded with thick holly bushes and pine trees. But she could just make out two very high, twisty chimneys, and a turret poking up on the corner.

"Looks more like a house for a ghost, than a scientist," Lucie said to Fang. "I wonder if Professor Pike does experiments in there? I wonder if he mixes up chemicals in test tubes. Imagine if one of them exploded..."

It was at this moment that Marcus jumped out from behind a gatepost. "Hah!" he yelled. "Gotcha!"

"Eek!" squeaked Lucie, jumping backwards. "What do you think you're doing?"

"Waiting for you," said Marcus. "And that animal you're talking to. Oh yes — I heard you — so no point denying it. But it can't *talk* you know, Lucie, however much you go wittering on." Marcus paused a few moments, staring at her with narrowed eyes. "*Or can it?*"

"What do you mean?" asked Lucie. She felt like a hand had taken hold of her stomach, and was squeezing it hard.

"Nothing," said Marcus. "Of course, it's ridiculous to think that a dog might talk." He paused. "About as ridiculous as thinking it might not even *be* a dog." He paused again. "That it might be a WOLF."

Lucie said not a word. But a wave of red swept across her cheeks. She dared not look at Fang.

"Ridiculous, of course," Marcus said. "Only if it *were* true...well, that would be interesting, wouldn't it? I wonder what would happen then? If people found out? I expect they would give the wolf to a scientist to study in their laboratory. Maybe to Professor Pike. Because *I* happen to know that Professor Pike *isn't* the kind of scientist who studies chemicals in test tubes. Mum mentioned it once. Professor Pike studies *animals.*" He paused again. "Cuts them up into little pieces I expect..."

Lucie gave a cry. Then she flew at Marcus. But before she could punch him in the middle of his smug, spiteful face, as she badly wanted to do, Fang grabbed the bottom of her skirt with her teeth and pulled her back.

Lucie swallowed, and tried to stay calm.

"What d'you want, Marcus?" she asked, from between gritted teeth.

"Meet me after school today. Between the gates and the After School Club. And bring that thing with you." He pointed at Fang.

"She's not a thing!"

Marcus shrugged.

"What if I don't?" said Lucie.

"Oh, I think you will. Unless you want everyone to know what *I* know about that DOG of yours. Beginning with Mr Dundas." Mr Dundas was the school Head Teacher.

Without waiting for an answer, Marcus turned and made off down the street, whistling.

"Thanks for stopping me hitting him," said Lucie in a shaky voice. "It wouldn't have helped."

"He'd just have hit you back," said Fang, "and he's stronger than you. Then I probably would have bitten him, even though I promised I wouldn't —"

"It would have only caused more trouble," Lucie agreed. "We'll just have to meet him. I wonder what he wants?"

"No good I expect. But I'll be with you," said Fang.

That was some comfort, anyway.

CHAPTER TEN
Emergency!

All through school that day, Marcus kept shooting Lucie mean looks. And all through school that day, Lucie kept wondering what it was he wanted.

At playtime, Lucie's teacher kept her back.

"Is anything the matter, Lucie?" asked Miss Singh kindly. "You seem very distracted today."

Lucie liked Miss Singh. For a moment she was tempted to confide in her. Then she imagined herself saying, "Marcus Mainwaring has found out that my dog is really a talking wolf, and is threatening to tell everybody so she can be sent to a zoo or cut up in a laboratory," and she knew she couldn't.

"There's nothing wrong really, Miss Singh," she said.

As she was leaving the classroom, she nearly bumped into Marcus, listening at the door.

"You sneaky sneak, Marcus!" said Lucie. "Why don't you mind your own business?"

"That would suit you, wouldn't it," sneered Marcus. "You and that ugly brute of yours." He turned away. "I'll see you after school. You'd better be there."

"I don't know about that," said Lucie.

He turned round again. "What do you mean?"

"Well — what's the point? What's in it for me?"

"I already told you. If you don't come I'm going to tell."

"But you might do that anyway," Lucie pointed out. "I'll tell you what — I'll come but only if you promise never, ever to tell anyone that Wolfie is a wolf." Lucie was not sure that she trusted Marcus to keep a promise, but she thought it worth a try.

"All right," said Marcus at last.

"You promise?"

"Yes."

"Then say it."

"I promise not to tell anyone that Wolfie is a wolf."

"On Gnasher's life?"

"On Gnasher's life."

"All right then," said Lucie. "I'll see you later."

She felt a bit better, even though she was not sure she could trust Marcus to keep a promise. She would have felt much worse if she had seen his face as he walked away. He was smirking. *Give him to next door's dog*, his mother had said. Well, Marcus was not prepared to give up Gnasher. He had a much better plan.

* * *

Directly school finished Marcus raced to the After School Club. It met in a building separate from the main school next to the school gates. Lots of children whose parents were still working went there. At the moment, though, it was still quiet.

The staff who ran the club always gave out drinks and snacks to the children. And for that reason it often had another visitor too.

"Hey kitty!" called Marcus. "Puss, puss, puss!"

From around the corner of the building came a little orange cat. It stood for a moment, hesitating. "Mew!" it called. Then it ran towards Marcus, expecting its usual saucer of milk.

Marcus crouched down and held out a hand. The cat came closer. And closer. When it was close enough he grabbed it.

"Mew!" said the little cat indignantly.

Marcus tucked it under his jacket.

* * *

Lucie also left school as quickly as possible and went to meet Fang at the gates. Almost immediately they saw Marcus coming towards them.

"Hey, Lucie," yelled a voice. It was Alex, waving at them. He was holding the hand of his little sister, Grace, while their mother chatted to another parent.

"Why's *he* always sticking his nose in?" muttered Marcus. "Ignore him! Look, I've something to show you."

He beckoned her a little way from the main crush by the gates. With extreme suspicion, Lucie and Fang followed. "What is it, Marcus?" Lucie asked.

"This!" Suddenly Marcus flung back his jacket. There was the little orange cat, clinging desperately with its claws to his shirt.

"Here," said Marcus to Fang with an evil grin. "I've brought you a playmate."

The little cat made mewling noises as Marcus wrenched it away from his shirt and held it out to Fang.

Lucie just stared. She was frozen with terror. She waited for Fang to snap up the cat. After all, Fang was a wolf. How would she be able to resist when it was right under her nose?

Around them, heads were turning. All the parents

and children were now staring at Fang and the little orange cat.

Fang opened her mouth very wide. Her lips curled back. Her pointed teeth gleamed white against her long, pink tongue...

Then she finished yawning and sat down to scratch her hind leg.

Lucie heaved a sigh of relief. The watching parents and children did the same. Only Marcus was disappointed. Scowling, he dropped the cat.

Unfortunately *somebody* was still terrified that Fang would go for the cat. And that was the cat itself! As soon as Marcus let go it went streaking across the pavement — and straight into the road.

Now cats are quick and this one must have had a sixth sense for cars. It was across the road in a flash of orange, and safe on the opposite side. But meanwhile something even worse happened. While everyone was still staring at Fang, or else the cat, little Grace Beamer went toddling into the road.

"Pussy Tat!" she cried. "Pussy Tat!"

A blue car was coming straight towards her.

Lucie noticed first. "Fang!" she screamed. "*Do something!*"

Everything happened very fast. While the children

and parents were still staring — almost as if they had been put under a spell — Fang bounded into the road. With a swish of her tail, she seized Grace in her mouth, and leapt for the opposite pavement. The car's brakes squealed. Grace's mother squealed louder — then fell in a faint. Marcus squealed too (this was because Alex had just thumped him). Then it seemed like everybody was squealing at once.

Everybody except for Grace. "Nice Doggy," she said, patting Fang on the nose. "Woof woof!"

CHAPTER ELEVEN
The Wolf-Dog

Fang was a heroine. And yet although she was famous in the school, and everybody was proud of her, and Lucie's parents were delighted with her, Lucie was in more danger of losing her than ever before.

Luckily Lucie had no idea of this — yet.

The next day there was a story in the local newspaper.

Super-Dog Rescues Baby!

There was drama at Acorn Primary School yesterday when toddler Grace Beamer, 3, was almost crushed under the wheels of a car. Grace had chased a cat onto the street just outside the school gates. As parents and children watched in horror, a huge hound leapt onto the street and dragged Grace to safety.

Wolfie

Grace's mother said, "My attention was distracted for just a moment, but that was enough. I will never forget the dog that saved Grace. I will always be grateful to her."

Grace and her mother had been waiting for Grace's brother Alex to come out of school. Alex said, "Wolfie belongs to a girl in my school. Everyone loves Wolfie. They'll love her even more now. She is the best dog ever."

Head teacher Mr Dundas said, "We are all so relieved that Grace is unhurt. We will be reconsidering our safety policies for going-home time."

Lucie read the story to Fang, who did not seem terribly interested. "You're a hero!" Lucie told her. "I mean *heroine*. Or should I say *wolferine* —"

"Don't you call *me* a wolverine!" said Fang, mishearing. "I'm not anything like one of those weaselly creatures. And stop waving that newspaper at me. We wolves aren't like you humans — always hankering to get our picture in the paper."

"That's good," said Lucie, "because your picture isn't *in* the paper."

But secretly Lucie thought it would be lovely if it was. And the newspaper editor must have thought the same thing, because the next day when Lucie came out of school a photographer was waiting. He rushed up and started taking pictures of Fang from all angles.

"My name's Jeb Jevons," he said, FLASH FLASH "from the Courier," FLASH FLASH. "Thought we should get some shots," FLASH "of the super-dog," FLASH "that saved the little lass," FLASH FLASH "don't you think?"

Fang did not like the flashes. She kept turning her back or trying to hide behind Lucie. But the camera was clicking so quickly that Jeb Jevons must have got several shots.

Some parents and children came to watch.

"What sort of dog is it?" asked Jeb Jevons, as Fang pulled back her ears and showed him her teeth. "What a set of gnashers! Looks almost like a wolf!"

Alex was standing close by. "Well, there's wolf blood in her," he said proudly. "Isn't there, Lucie?"

It was an unlucky remark. Lucie hesitated, not sure what to say. Some of the parents began to look

nervous. They began grabbing their children, and pulling them away.

"Wolf blood, eh?" said Jeb Jevons. "That's interesting. *Very* interesting."

"Well, actually —" began Lucie. She was going to say it was all a misunderstanding — that of course Wolfie wasn't a wolf. But it was too late. Jeb Jevons climbed into his car and drove away.

Alex and Lucie were left staring at each other on the empty pavement. "Wonder why they all ran off like that?" asked Alex.

"I don't know," said Lucie. "Come on, Wolfie. Let's get home."

* * *

Next day there was a huge picture of Fang in the paper. On the front page too. It was one of the ones where she was showing her teeth. Underneath was written:

Wolf-Dog At Large

You might not want to meet this creature walking down your street. Especially as we've been told

it really is part wolf! But it was Wolfie the Wolf-Dog that pulled toddler Grace to safety from under the wheels of a car on Tuesday. Three Big Howls For Wolfie!

Fang just yawned when Lucie showed it to her, then started chewing the newspaper.

Others reacted differently.

That afternoon, when Lucie came out of school, there was an empty circle of pavement all around Fang. It seemed nobody wanted to stand too close to the "Wolf-Dog". From a safe distance the grown-ups muttered amongst themselves.

The odd word floated over to Lucie. "Enormous" and "teeth" and "wolf blood" and "savage". Then she heard somebody say clearly, "Really, it shouldn't be allowed!"

Lucie ran to Fang and hugged her.

"Oh Wolfie!" she cried. "It's not fair." Then she turned on those around her. "Cowards!" she shouted. "She won't hurt you!"

She was about to march off when she heard a stern voice behind her. "Lucie Firkettle! What is the meaning of this?" Lucie turned to see Mr Dundas, the Head of the whole school, glaring down at her.

Lucie swallowed. She had hardly ever spoken to Mr Dundas before. "What do you mean?" she asked.

Mr Dundas pointed at Fang. "Is this the dog that has been causing all the fuss?"

"Fuss!" Lucie was so furious she forgot to be shy. "*Fuss*? She saved Grace's life, if that's what you mean!"

"Lucie!" Mr Dundas frowned. "Don't be impertinent! Now tell me: is it true this animal is part wolf?"

There was a long silence. All the parents and children waited to hear what Lucie would say.

"*No*," she said, as definitely as she could. After all Fang was *not* part wolf. She was *all* wolf.

"But you said she had wolf blood in her," said Marcus, who was hovering close by as usual. "I heard you tell Alex so, on the very first day of term!"

"You little creep!" said Alex, scowling. "Don't take any notice!"

"But it's true, isn't it?" said one of the mothers nervously. "I heard this boy —" she pointed at Alex — "say exactly the same thing to that newspaper man yesterday."

"But not to get Wolfie into trouble!" said Alex. "I think Wolfie's great!"

"Hmm," said Mr Dundas irritably. He was still

frowning at Fang. Fang, meanwhile, was sitting peacefully on the pavement, as if all the commotion bothered her not at all.

Suddenly Lucie remembered how she had calmed everybody down in the playground in the park. It had worked then, so why not now? "My goodness!" she cried in a high, bright voice. "Do you really believe all these stories about wolf blood? How ridiculous! I mean, whoever heard of a wolf at school! Ha ha! Hee hee!"

But although she chortled and chuckled until she felt she was going blue in the face, this time it did not work. Nobody joined in. They just went on staring at Fang.

"Look at the size of its paws!" said somebody.

"And its teeth!"

"And its pointy ears!"

"And its tail!"

"Bite you soon as look at you."

"Savage, that's what it is —"

Fang began to get annoyed. She drew her lips back in a half-snarl. This did not help.

Lucie felt close to tears. "Come on Fang," she said shakily. And although she could hear Mr Dundas calling her back, she paid no attention, but ran for home.

CHAPTER TWELVE
Fang in Danger

When she got home, Lucie was surprised to find her parents sitting at the kitchen table, drinking coffee, with very worried faces.

"Hello," she said.

"Oh...err...hello Lucie." They avoided her eyes. Her dad fiddled with his coffee spoon.

"What's the matter?" she asked

"Nothing," said Dad. "At least, nothing serious. At least, I don't think it's serious. Err, I don't think."

"We've just had a phone call from Mr Dundas," said Mum. "He's very concerned. It seems there's been a lot of complaints...about Wolfie. He says some people are saying...well, they're saying that Wolfie might be a wolf. Ridiculous, I know." But Mum didn't laugh at how ridiculous it was. She just looked at Fang. It was a worried look.

"But Mum, it's not fair! All Wolfie did was save someone's life."

"I know. But Mr Dundas seems to think that if

Wolfie hadn't been outside of the school in the first place then none of it would have happened..."

"It wouldn't have happened if Marcus Mainwaring hadn't been up to his nasty tricks! Why don't they get rid of *him*?"

"It doesn't work that way. And Mr Dundas says that unless we can prove that Wolfie is not a wolf, then he is going to report the whole matter to the police."

There was a long pause. Everybody looked at Fang, who sat quietly on the kitchen floor.

"She can't be a wolf..." whispered Mum "...can she?"

Lucie said, "It was me who said she was, right at the start. And you both said she wasn't. Didn't you, Dad?"

"Did I?" asked Dad vaguely.

"Yes!"

"Oh."

"So why don't you just tell Mr Dundas the same thing!"

"Oh, we will, we will," said Dad. But he didn't sound very sure. Then he put his cup down and said in a falsely hearty voice, "I'm sure there's nothing to worry about! Don't you give it another thought, Lucie. Just leave the whole matter to us."

* * *

But of course Lucie did think about it — all the time. Her parents wouldn't talk to her any more about it, but they kept having muttered conversations when they thought she couldn't hear. When she asked what was going on they just said, "don't worry" and "everything's under control."

This did not comfort Lucie one bit.

"Oh Fang, what do you think will happen now?" Lucie asked as they sat together in Lucie's bedroom.

"Who knows? But I am afraid they will decide I'm a wolf, and get rid of me."

Tears sprung into Lucie's eyes.

"It's not fair! You've *always* been a wolf! Nobody minded before. Nobody even noticed."

"The trouble is, when I saved that child, people paid attention. For the first time, they really *looked*. Close up. Using their *eyes*. Human beings often do not notice what is right under their noses. But when they do start looking...well..." Fang shrugged. "Even human beings are not *completely* stupid."

"But what can we do?"

"I don't know," said Fang. "The trouble is, I don't understand human beings well enough. I don't know what would make people change their minds."

"Can't you use your Magic Powers?" asked Lucie desperately.

Fang snorted. "There are no Magic Powers that can change what goes on in peoples' heads! If there were, I could rule the world!"

Lucie sat silently for a while. Then she said, "Maybe we could change what goes on in Mum and Dad's heads. Maybe that would be enough..."

"How would we do that?"

"What happens if *you* talk to Mum and Dad? You could tell them that you are a wolf, but you're a nice wolf, a talking wolf, who doesn't eat people."

"*Nice?*" said Fang, who seemed a bit offended. "You make me sound like a golden retriever. And I could eat people if I wanted to. If only I'd eaten Marcus, none of this would have happened."

"Whatever you do, don't say that! Just explain that you are kind and loyal and you don't do anyone any harm...except rabbits." Lucie considered. "In fact, don't mention the rabbits."

"It's a good idea," said Fang kindly, "but unfortunately it's impossible."

"Why?"

"Because we Talking Wolves have sworn a Solemn

Vow of Secrecy. We never speak to any grown human being if we can help it."

"But why?" asked Lucie.

"It's too dangerous. If humans knew we could talk they would lock us up, and put us in laboratories, and study us and do experiments. Maybe they'd cut us up to see how we work. And they wouldn't stop until they had hunted down the whole of our kind."

"Mum and Dad wouldn't tell."

"Maybe not. But I still can't risk it."

"Then why did you talk to me?"

"You are only one person. And you're a child. Nobody would ever listen to you. Besides," added Fang, "I liked you. You smelled right."

Lucie considered. She still thought that her parents might help, if only they knew the truth.

"All right then, what if I told them?" she said at last. "I know they're grow-ups, but still...they are nice, really...surely they'd understand."

Fang wrinkled her nose. "You can try."

Later that day Lucie went into her Dad's study, where he was working away on his computer as usual.

"Dad," said Lucie, "what would you say if I told you that Wolfie wasn't a dog, she was really a wolf?"

Wolfie

"Eh?" said Dad. "What's that?"

Lucie repeated her question. "And not just any wolf," she added. "A *talking* wolf?"

"Hmm," said Dad, rubbing his nose as he did when he was thinking. (Although whether he was thinking about his computer code or what Lucie had said it was hard to know.) "Do you think it's the sort of thing you're likely to say?"

"I'm not sure," said Lucie, "but what if I did?"

"Hmm. I suppose I'd say you'd been reading too many storybooks. Or maybe I'd call up the zoo — yes, they ought to be able to put you straight."

Lucie turned and quietly left the room, and Dad went back to his computer and immediately forgot the whole conversation.

Later on she asked her mother the same questions.

"A talking wolf!" cried her mother. "Quelle idée! Lucie, are you feeling all right?" And she put a hand to Lucie's head. "You must have a fever to say such things. Come and lie down right now."

"Err...forget it," Lucie mumbled.

There was only one person who was still on her side, and that was Alex. Of course, Alex did not know that Fang — or Wolfie, as he thought of her — could talk. But he was almost as worried about what was going to happen to her as Lucie was. He also felt terrible that he had got Wolfie into so much trouble by saying that she had wolf blood, even though Lucie kept telling him it wasn't his fault.

The two of them spent ages trying to work out what to do next.

"What we need," he said one day during lunch break, "is someone like a vet or a zoo keeper to say definitely that Wolfie is not a wolf. Maybe they could sign a certificate. What do you think? Shall we take her to the zoo and see if they'll say she's not?"

"The trouble is," said Lucie, "what if they say she IS?"

They both shivered. It was true that the weather had gone very cold lately, but that was not the reason. They were thinking of what might happen next.

That evening Lucie and Fang sat in Lucie's bedroom, talking. Lucie was supposed to be doing her homework, but it lay forgotten on the rug.

"What do you think's going on?" Lucie asked Fang. "I know something is. But Mum and Dad won't tell me anything."

There was a pause. Then Fang said, "I think they are planning to take me to a vet."

"No! Why do you think so?"

"I overheard them talking while you were at school. Of course, they don't know that I can understand what they say."

"And a vet — " Lucie began, then stopped.

"— will know that I'm not a dog," Fang said.

At that moment they heard footsteps on the stairs. They both fell silent, and the next moment Mum came into the room. Lucie leapt to her feet.

"You mustn't get rid of Wolfie!" she cried.

"Sweetheart," said Mum. "You mustn't get into a state." She came and sat down on the bed and put her arm around Lucie. "We've already told you we're going to deal with this."

"Are you going to take Wolfie to a vet?"

"We're making enquiries. And after all, Lucie, Mr Dundas does have a point. I phoned Uncle Joe, to find out more about Wolfie. And would you believe it, he doesn't know anything about her! He bought her from somebody he met in the street. Imagine that! We can't even ask her old owner about her. So really, it's only sensible to find out more about her...before we decide whether to keep her."

Lucie was so horrified that for a moment she could find no words. "But we *have* to keep her!" she croaked at last.

Mum hugged her tight. "You're our little girl and we love you and we have to do what's best for you. After all," she went on brightly, "it's not long till Christmas! Who knows — maybe Santa will bring you a new pet!" She got up. "Just one more thing," she added, "until we find out for sure, Dad and I think it might be better if Wolfie sleeps downstairs."

Lucie found her voice. "What are you so worried about? That she might save my life in the night?"

But there was no point arguing. There never was when her parents had an idea fixed in their heads. Fang gently licked her palm. Lucie was quiet. Her Mum gave her a big kiss, and then took Fang downstairs.

That night Lucie lay in bed, staring at the empty patch of rug where Fang usually slept. It felt strange without her. Lucie was used to the sound of her breathing. She was used to looking across and seeing her in the night.

Lucie imagined going to sleep without Fang, maybe for the rest of her life.

A tear trickled down her cheek.

Night drew in. Outside the air grew colder. Downstairs, Lucie's parents turned off the TV and went up to bed. The full moon rose, sending its light

through the gap in Lucie's curtains to lie in a silver
bar across her bed.

The church clock chimed eleven. Then twelve.

It was so quiet you could have heard a pin drop.

Or a wolf, breathing.

CHAPTER THIRTEEN
Midnight Again

Lucie tossed and turned. In her dreams she was wandering deep in a snowy forest. She could hear wolves howling in the distance. For a moment she woke up, and thought she could still hear them. Then she drifted back into a troubled sleep.

Suddenly she sat up, wide awake. Two eyes were gleaming at her.

"Fang!" whispered Lucie.

Fang laid a paw on Lucie's arm. Then she glanced at the window. "The moon is full," she said. "And Wolves are Roaming."

"Roaming where?" Lucie whispered. Fang did not answer.

"Oh, Fang," Lucie whispered. "You're not leaving?"

Fang was still gazing at the moon. She seemed to be thinking.

"Are you brave enough to come too?" she asked at last. "Are you brave enough to Roam with Wolves? Are you ready to seek out their Wisdom?"

"Yes," said Lucie. "But," she added, "we won't go

forever? I mean, I know my parents are sometimes stupid and annoying, but I can't leave them *forever*. They would be so upset."

"One night should be enough. Either we find a way or we don't. Climb on my back, She-Child."

Lucie slipped out of bed and put on her warm dressing-gown and slippers. Then she climbed onto Fang's back. It felt very odd. Lucie had once tried riding a pony. But riding a wolf felt completely different.

"Hold tight," said Fang. "Don't worry about pulling my fur. You won't hurt me. And grip tight with your heels. If you are *very* frightened," she added, "it might be best to shut your eyes."

Lucie *was* a bit frightened then, especially as the next thing Fang did was to leap onto the window sill. To her astonishment, Lucie saw that it was snowing. Snowflakes swirled through the air and down onto the darkened garden, as if someone was emptying bags of feathers.

Fang pushed at the window with her paw, and even though Lucie had been sure it was locked, it came open.

Then Fang crouched low, gathered her strength... and leapt into the night.

The air roared around Lucie's ears. *This must be a dream*, she thought. *Because if Fang really did jump out of the window, we'd have hit the ground by now and that would be the end of us!*

But the cold snow on her face was real. So was the owl that almost flew into them, with an alarmed "Tu-Whoo!" And the enormous drop beneath her, that Lucie saw when she dared to look down — yes, that was real too.

"We are flying!" yelled Lucie. "We're really flying!"

"I know," said Fang. "No need to make so much racket."

Lucie gazed around at the steep rooftops and the swirling snow. She began to laugh with surprise and delight.

"Don't do that," said Fang. "You'll fall off."

So Lucie sat quietly and tried to see what she could recognise. They were circling round over the old professor's house. Lucie had always thought it looked like a haunted house, with its turret and twisted chimneys like tall, black candlesticks. It looked more haunted than ever in the snow.

They approached the church clock.

"What's that?" Lucie cried, as a black shadow squeaked.

Wolfie

"Just a bat," said Fang.

They were gaining height now. The moon was rushing towards them. The air round Lucie's ears grew into a wind. Fang was flying — but it felt more as if she were running.

And the strange thing was that although Lucie was in the middle of a snowstorm, and in only her night things and dressing-gown, she felt warm as toast.

A plaintive howl echoed through the sky. Fang lifted her head and howled too. Then she ran through the air even faster than before.

For a while Lucie was so giddy that she just clutched at Fang and shut her eyes. She felt they must have travelled miles and miles. The air was much colder, and there were no traffic sounds.

When she was able to look down again, she saw that they had not come so far after all. They were over the park.

At least, Lucie thought it was the park. But she could not see the playground. Nor the bandstand. Nor the café by the lake. Nor any of the concrete paths.

All she could see were trees, with wide, snow-covered spaces running between them; the lake; and the darkness of the ravine.

Wolfie

"Is that the park?" she asked Fang. "I mean, it *looks* like the park. But then in another way it doesn't."

"It *is* the park," said Fang. "But it was a meeting place for us wolves long before you humans came and put your walls and fences round it."

Fang began to run fast again. It had stopped snowing. The sky was full of stars. Dad had once told Lucie that it was hard to see the stars clearly nowadays because of all the streetlights, but tonight they shone and shimmered like anything.

Suddenly there was a great noise of howling. It sounded like hundreds and hundreds of wolves.

Then there were other shapes running beside them. White or grey, black or brown, even tinged with red, they raced through the night, with their tails streaming behind them. Wolves. After a while they were all of them running along the ground (although Lucie could not remember actually landing) and weaving through trees, and leaping streams and boulders.

Lucie was breathless, certain she had never travelled so fast in her life. She should be terrified — yet she was filled with a wild joy and excitement.

At last they entered a wide, snow-covered clearing. Many wolves were gathered there. Fang walked among them, pausing to greet wolf after wolf, nodding and bowing. The wolves were very polite. Although none of them were carrying children, they did not ask about Lucie, or stare.

Then, as they approached one side of the clearing, Lucie saw a wolf sitting near a tall fir tree. Immediately, she sensed that this wolf was special.

Fang lowered her head. She approached the new wolf very slowly. When she was a body-length away, she flattened herself to the ground.

The new wolf was very, very old. It had a lean, white muzzle and milky-white eyes. Two younger wolves stood on either side, like guard-wolves. Lucie sensed that Fang respected this wolf greatly.

"Greetings, Oh Fang-That-Bites-Sharp-In-The Forest," said the old wolf, in a husky voice. "Who is this Human Child? And why have you broken our custom to bring her here among us?"

CHAPTER FOURTEEN
Silver Paw

"Oh great and august He-Wolf, most esteemed Lord Silver Paw," Fang began, "this is Lucie, a young human, what they call a girl. I have been living with her family these past months. She has shown me great kindness and hospitality. Indeed, I would go so far as to say that we are friends."

"Friends!" said the old wolf, and he looked at Lucie with great attention. Lucie blushed. Then Silver Paw turned back to Fang. "Then what is it that troubles you?" he asked. "For something does."

Fang sighed. "Recently I saved a human child. Otherwise it would have been squashed to a pulp under the wheels of one of their infernal machines— one of those foul-smelling "cars" they like so much. But doing this deed attracted attention. And hostility. Now it seems that I must leave."

Silver Paw wrinkled his nose. "Praise might be expected for saving a child. Not hostility. Were it not discourteous to our guest, I might observe that the ways of humans are strange — even ungrateful."

"Yes," said Lucie shyly. "You're right. But I don't think people *mean* to be ungrateful. Really I don't."

"Then what do they mean?"

"I think they're frightened. And it makes them stupid."

Silver Paw considered. "It may be so. Often your kind — humankind — acts stupidly towards ours. Yet maybe fear is the reason." Silver Paw turned back to Fang. "Still, I do not see what *I* can do. You must seek out another refuge, that is all."

At this, tears sprung into Lucie's eyes. "Oh please, great august Silver Paw — I'm so sorry, I can't remember all of your names! Please help us! I never had a friend like Fang before. I'll do anything!"

Silver Paw fixed his eyes on Lucie. It was hard for the small girl not to look away from his deep wolf-stare, but somehow she did not. She kept her chin raised, and her eyes wide open, and she hoped and hoped.

"Will you then become a True Friend to the Wolves?" asked Silver Paw. "It is no small thing."

"Yes! Oh, yes!"

"Then step aside one moment. I must speak with Fang alone."

Lucie followed one of the guard-wolves. She sat down on the grass, and crossed her fingers and hugged her knees.

Meanwhile Silver Paw beckoned to Fang. The two wolves rubbed noses, then sat down facing each other.

"Is it wise," asked Silver Paw at last, "to take this child into your heart? Certainly, she is appealing — for a *human*. Intelligent even. But think, Fang, she will grow. And the grown ones of her species are almost always stupid, it seems to me."

"Lucie is a special child," said Fang. "Not every child can hear when we speak. Or not so as to understand. Lucie does. I think she will always be special."

"All the same, would it not be simpler to leave her and find another home?"

Fang shook her head.

Silver Paw said, "Bring the child back to me."

Fang fetched Lucie. Together the wolf and the girl stood facing Silver Paw.

"So, child," said Silver Paw. "It is not our custom to bring humans among us, nor to give them help. But I am told that you are a friend to Fang."

"Oh yes. I will never let her down, I promise!"

"It is a serious matter, such a promise. But the truth is I do not know if I can help you. For the cause of your trouble lies among humans. So the solution must be found there too. If I am to help you then you yourself must point the way."

"Oh," cried Lucie, tears of disappointment in her eyes.

"Perhaps it would be better if Fang left for the present. Then the other humans might forget their fears. She could come back later to find out. If so... good. If not..." Silver Paw shrugged.

"No!" cried Lucie. "She mustn't go away!"

"Then is there anything you can tell me that might help?"

The old wolf's eyes bored into Lucie. He was expecting something. But what?

"I don't know what to tell you," said Lucie desperately. "Except — except that I know that Fang must never leave Acorn Avenue!"

There was a long pause after those words. Lucie felt close to tears. But at her words something changed in the old wolf's face. Something flickered in his milky eyes.

"*Acorn Avenue*, you say?"

"Yes. It's where I live."

"I see. Yes. That might be important."

"Really?" asked Lucie, astonished.

Silver Paw was staring into the distance. Lucie had the feeling he was listening hard to something, even though there was nothing to hear except the wind. But then, maybe a wolf could hear things in the wind that a human could not.

At last he said, "Maybe I *can* help you. Or rather, I can help you to help yourself. But you alone must find the answer. For the solution lies not with us wolves, but in the human world."

"What am I to do?"

"Listen." And the old wolf began to speak in a sing-song voice.

> *"The task begins at your own front door*
> *For answer follow your own right paw*
> *Human knowledge is what you need*
> *Written in form that humans read."*

"Is that it? But what does it mean?" cried Lucie hopelessly.

"You must work it out for yourself. Thus proving that you at least, of all your kind, are not stupid. If you succeed then you will have shown yourself a true friend to Fang and to wolves. You will become a Cub of our Pack — the first human ever to be so chosen. Come here."

Then Fang nudged Lucie forward with her nose, until she stood between the paws of the old wolf.

Silver Paw breathed softly on Lucie. Very gently he licked Lucie's forehead.

"Good luck, Little Cub," he said. "May you complete your task."

The snow was swirling again. The wolves were still milling around their clearing but now it was as if they were performing a beautiful dance. They wove in and out in intricate patterns, their tails flowing behind them. Lucie's head spun, and even the stars seemed to be dancing...the wind was rushing past her ears...

Suddenly Lucie sat up with a start. It was still dark. The church clock was striking six.

CHAPTER FIFTEEN
Following the Right Paw

"Of course it must have been a dream," said Lucie to Fang. "I mean really! Flying out of the window to a Wolf Meet in the park! I *know* I dreamt it. I did, didn't I?"

"If you're so sure —" Fang yawned — "then why are you asking *me*?"

"Because I'm *not* sure, of course!" Lucie shouted. "And because I want it to be true. I *need* it to be true! Silver Paw's advice is the only hope we have!"

They were walking round and round the garden in the snow, rather like Pooh and Piglet pursuing the Woozle, Lucie thought. But there was nowhere else they could talk. They were no longer allowed to go to the park alone.

"Then let's just assume it's true," Fang suggested.

"But then what? I don't understand." Lucie quoted:
The task begins at your own front door
For answer follow your own right paw
Human knowledge is what you need
Written in form that humans read.

But what does it mean?"

Fang shrugged.

"A lot of help you are!" said Lucie crossly. "I know Silver Paw said it was for me to solve, but still...you might at least make a suggestion!"

There was a distant shout. "Lucie, time for school!"

"Oh, bother!" Lucie leapt up. "Bother, bother, bother!"

But when school was over Lucie returned in a calmer mood. Fang was still prowling about the garden in snow that was rapidly turning into slush.

"I thought it best not to meet you," said Fang. "With all the fuss there's been recently."

"You're right," said Lucie, sitting herself on her swing. "I'm afraid Mr Dundas hasn't forgotten. He was standing by the school gates when I came out. I'm sure it was just so he could check you weren't there. Dad came to meet me, and he asked Dad what he had decided to do with you, and Dad said he would tell him tomorrow. I think it must be tomorrow they've made the appointment with the vet."

Fang nodded. Lucie stared miserably at the chestnut tree. The melted snow was dripping from the bare branches onto the ground. The drops looked a bit like tears.

"I've decided," Lucie began. "I'm going to —"

"Wait!" said Fang quickly. "Someone's coming!"

They both fell silent. After a while Lucie heard what Fang's more sensitive ears had heard already: the crunch of footsteps. *Someone* was coming round the side of the house.

"Marcus!" Lucie whispered.

"No. The smell's not right. It's not got that nasty undertone of weasel and mouldy cheese." She sniffed. "I think it's the nice boy."

Alex appeared around the corner of the house. "Oh, there you are," he said. "Your Mum and Dad said you'd be in the garden." He stood next to the swing, looking awkward. "I just wanted to see if I could help," he burst out suddenly. "I've begged Mum to let *us* take Wolfie if you can't keep her, but she says we've only a tiny garden and Dad is allergic to dogs..."

"Don't worry," said Lucie. "I want Wolfie to stay here, anyway."

"I wish there was something I could do."

"There is," said Lucie. "You can go round and see Marcus."

Alex blinked. "*What?*"

"I need you to keep him out of the way. You see,

he doesn't go to After School Club on Wednesdays."
Lucie flushed. "I can't really explain, but I want to
try something — something somebody told me that
might help Wolfie. Only I don't want Marcus sticking
his big nose in and messing things up."

"Leave it to me," said Alex. He looked a lot more
cheerful now he had something to do. Then he said,
"Wait a minute. Won't Marcus be suspicious if I go
round? He knows I don't like him."

"Tell him you're sounding him out to be goalie
for the school team," said Lucie. "That'll do the trick."

Alex snorted. "Have you *seen* Marcus play
football?"

"No. But he's such a big-head he'll believe you."

"All right. I'll get him to practise stopping some
shots. Good luck."

He ran off. Lucie heaved a sigh. "Thank goodness!
That was the one thing I was most worried about.
Come on, Fang!"

"Come where?" Fang asked.

"To do what the rhyme says. I don't know what
it *means*, but it's our only hope, so I've decided I'm
going to do exactly what it says. I'm going to follow
my right paw!" She looked down at her right foot.
"That way!" She started off across the slushy ground.

Fang coughed. "That way seems to lead into a wall."

"Oh." Lucie's face fell. "Then maybe we could get a ladder. Or tunnel underneath..."

"We wolves have a saying," Fang remarked. "*Start at your own front door.*"

Lucie hit her forehead. "I am stupid! Of course that's what the rhyme says too. *The Task begins at your own Front Door.* Come on!"

As it happened, Lucie's house had a porch that stuck out from the main house, and the door was on the left hand side of this porch. Which meant, Lucie soon discovered, that if she came out of the front door, and immediately went right (so following her right paw — or foot) she arrived at the front gate.

"We're on the right track I'm sure!" said Lucie.

"You mean the right *paw*," said Fang.

Then Lucie followed her right foot again and set off along Acorn Avenue. It was beginning to get dark, and the streetlights had come on. Soon Lucie was walking through the slush next to the railings at the front of Professor Pike's house. Lucie's feet dragged. She had always hated this house — even before she had found out that Professor Pike was the kind of scientist who liked chopping animals up into tiny bits.

Lucie's feet grew slower and slower until they reached the gate that led into Professor Pike's garden. Then they stopped altogether.

"Well?" Fang asked.

Lucie stood, hesitating. "I don't know," she said. "I don't see how the answer can possibly be here. Do you?"

Fang said nothing.

"I wish you wouldn't just look!" said Lucie.

She wanted to walk on. But just ahead of them was a corner where the wall stuck out and the pavement turned left. And if she turned left she would no longer be following her right paw.

"I mean," Lucie gabbled, "I don't think Silver Paw could have meant *this* house. Nobody lives here but a grumpy old professor!"

Fang still said nothing.

"I've always thought this place was downright spooky!" Lucie declared. "I'm not going in — and that's final!"

"Then let's go on."

"But we can't, not if we want to follow our right paws! Besides I *know* this is the place! I — I can smell it somehow!"

"Ah, now you're talking like a sensible cub," said

Fang approvingly. "A clever wolf always trusts her nose."

"Yes, but whatever my nose says, the rest of me wants to run away as fast as possible!"

Fang laughed. At least, she made no sound, but Lucie could see from her eyes that she was laughing.

"And you're no help!" Lucie said.

As she stood, undecided, a gust of wind shook the tree behind her, and a twig came fluttering down. It landed in front of Lucie, between the two gateposts of Professor Pike's house.

"Look!" said Lucie. "It's an oak twig. I never noticed that tree was an oak before. And it has an acorn on it." Her eyes shone. "It's a sign! Don't you remember? It was when I said I lived on Acorn Avenue that Silver Paw said he could help. And now here is an acorn, showing the way!"

She lifted her chin. "We're going into Professor Pike's garden!"

CHAPTER SIXTEEN
The Den

Marcus Mainwaring was very intrigued by what he saw that afternoon from his bedroom window. First he saw Lucie and that horrible wolf-dog of hers sitting in her back garden. Then a new person turned up, and to his amazement he recognised Alex Beamer. What was *he* doing there? Why was he so friendly with a stupid squit like Lucie? Marcus scowled through his binoculars.

Then, almost as soon as he had arrived, Alex left. And a moment later, Lucie leapt up and started marching about the garden, before vanishing round the side of the house. Marcus ran to the landing window to see where she was going...

"Marcus!" shouted Mrs Mainwaring. "Someone to see you!"

"Bother!" said Marcus. But then he saw it was Alex.

"Hey, Alex," said Marcus, running down the stairs.

"Hi Marcus. Listen. I need to talk to you about something important."

"Oh yes?" asked Marcus as casually as he could manage.

"It's like this. We could really do with a new goalie for the school team. That Owen Birt isn't up to much. So — some of us thought you might be interested..."

"Of course, it's not exactly a surprise," said Marcus, sticking out his chest.

"Isn't it?"

"Actually, I was almost expecting it. Do you know, I saw you just now in Lucie Firkettle's back garden? I just happened to glance out of the window and there you were. And I thought to myself, I bet Alex has gone in there by mistake, looking for my house. I suppose I should have guessed."

"Err — yes."

"Of course, in some ways I'd *rather* play up front —"

"That's *my* position," said Alex firmly. "Come on. If you're interested let's go and try some practice shots before it gets too dark. D'you have a football? I forgot mine."

And with the prospect of playing on the school team before him, Marcus forgot all about the strange behaviour of Lucie Firkettle.

* * *

Meanwhile, Lucie was standing on the front doorstep of Professor Pike's house. Enormous bushes of spiky holly screened her from the road, while above her loomed the house, without a single light showing. Her heart was thumping, and even though she had Fang beside her, she was scared.

There was no bell, so she grasped the door knocker and banged as loud as she could.

As she let go she gasped.

"What is it?" murmured Fang.

"Look at the door knocker!"

It was in the shape of a wolf's head.

"Rather fetching," murmured Fang.

"And no more talking!" Lucie whispered. "Remember your vow!"

There was a long pause. It really did seem that Professor Pike might have died, or at least gone out for the day. During the wait, Lucie noticed a sign next to the door. She had not seen it before because of the ivy hanging over it. When she pushed the leaves away she could clearly read *The Den*.

"Odd name for a house," she murmured.

Lucie was about to hammer on the door again, when there was a scraping noise. It was as if someone were pulling back a very rusty bolt. Then there was a squeaking noise, as if someone were turning a very rusty key. Finally, ever so slowly, the door swung out towards them.

Lucie's hands were clenched so tight that her fingernails were pressing into her palms.

At first all Lucie could make out was the dim shape of a bent-over figure. It was leaning on a stick. Then it reached out a hand and a light snapped on. The harsh electric beam made Lucie jump.

"Oh!" she said, disappointed. For after all that worrying, there was nothing to see but an elderly lady, with a round pink face and white hair, dressed in a cardie and tartan skirt.

"Yes?" said the old lady.

"Can I speak to Professor Pike, please?"

"Yes?" said the old woman again.

"Well, then, can I?"

"Well — yes," said the old lady. "I've already said so."

"Then where is he?" demanded Lucie, losing patience. "Or are we just going to stand on this doorstep forever?"

The old lady drew herself up to her full height (which was not very high). "I *am* Professor Pike, you impertinent child! Now tell me what you want before I shut the door on you!"

"Oh!" gasped Lucie. She suddenly felt extremely silly.

"Well?"

"I'm sorry," Lucie stammered. "You see —" She was about to say *You don't look like the kind of person who cuts animals into tiny pieces*, but instead she said, "— you just look like somebody's granny."

"Grannies can be professors too, you know," Professor Pike told her rather sharply, "and vice versa, of course. Now what can I do for you?"

"The thing is, I'm not sure."

"Then I think we've wasted enough time!" Professor Pike began to shut the door. But before she could, Lucie put her foot in the gap.

"I'm ever so sorry. I know it must seem strange. But I really do need your help!"

"I'll give you five minutes," said the Professor. And to show she meant it, she looked at her watch.

Lucie could think of nothing else to do but to tell her the whole story. So she did. Or most of it anyway. She did not tell her the magic bits, or how Fang could talk. But she told how Uncle Joe had brought

Fang as a present, and Lucie had said that she was a wolf, only nobody would believe her. How Fang had proved herself a loyal friend and companion, and everybody had come to like her, including Lucie's parents. How Fang had accompanied Lucie to school each day, and how there had been no problems until Marcus had decided to play his mean and spiteful trick. How Fang had saved little Grace's life, only now, suddenly, everyone was wondering if she was a wolf after all, and saying that if she was she would have to go.

"And *someone* — someone kind — said you might help. I don't understand how. But if you can help, *please* do because I can't bear the thought of Fang going away!"

Lucie waited for Professor Pike to react. She thought she might stare in fear and horror at Fang. Or ask in her grumpy voice just what did Lucie expect *her* to do? Or even go into her house and slam the door. But Professor Pike did none of those things.

"Goodness gracious," said Professor Pike, "why didn't you explain all this at the start?"

"I don't understand."

"What *you* need, my dear, is my expert opinion.

Now why didn't you say so before? Let's go inside. It's much warmer — and I shall need my spectacles!"

Rather confused, Lucie followed Professor Pike into the house, with Fang beside her. They went down a very long, dark corridor, filled with very peculiar things. There was a sled on one wall, for example, and a picture of Professor Pike in a fur hat, and some glass cases full of bones. Lucie glanced at these nervously, and wondered if they were human or animal bones, and if Marcus had been right about Professor Pike after all.

Eventually Professor Pike showed them into her study, which was cosy — if extremely messy. All kinds of things were crammed into it. Lucie sat on an over-stuffed sofa, and Fang sat on the rug next to her, and they watched as Professor Pike hunted for her glasses. She looked under the newspaper, and behind the clock, and next to the computer on the desk, and on all the bookshelves (there were a *lot* of bookshelves) and behind a glass case full of more bones. Eventually she found them dangling by one ear-piece from a coat-hook on the door.

"Is that your gold medal?" asked Lucie shyly, pointing to the shiny medal on a red ribbon that was hanging from the same hook.

"That's right. I was wondering where it had got to." Professor Pike picked it up, looked around, then decided she might as well put it back on the hook.

"What did you get it for?"

"My research, of course."

"I don't really know what that is," Lucie admitted. "And I'm afraid I don't know what an expert opinion is either."

"My dear child," said the Professor, "what do you think I'm a professor of?"

"I don't know. Although I'm sure it's very clever and difficult," said Lucie quickly.

"Zoology. And my particular speciality is canines. All canines — but *especially* wolves. I take it you know that the wolf is the common name for *Canis Lupus*?" Lucie shook her head and the Professor tutted. "Well it is. And let me tell you, there is nobody in this country better placed to tell you whether this animal is a dog or a wolf than I am. And so — to work!"

The Professor had been polishing her spectacles on her cardigan as she spoke. Now she perched them on her nose. Then she stared very hard at Fang, as if she were seeing her for the first time. "Well, well," she said. "Well, well, *well*."

The Professor walked round Fang, examining her from every angle. Lucie fidgeted. A new worry nagged at her. A terrible worry. If the Professor really *did* know all about wolves...then surely she would see at once that Fang was a wolf and not a dog. What would happen then?

At last the Professor spoke.

"In all my born days," she said slowly, "I never expected to see this. Not in my own living-room!"

Lucie stared at her feet.

"The years I have spent studying wolves!" continued the Professor. "Pursuing them through the Rocky Mountains! Tracking them across the snow-covered Steppes! Once I spent an entire fortnight camped out in a blizzard, just so I could observe a single wolf den! I was lucky that a passing grizzly bear didn't happen to observe *me*! And now here in my own study..." She shook her head, speechless.

"Please!" begged Lucie. "Just tell me! Is she a wolf or a dog?"

"A dog?" echoed the Professor. "A *dog*? My goodness no. I never saw a specimen of *Canis Familiaris* that looked like this. Look at the size of the head. Whoever saw a dog with a head that big?

And then there's the paws. And the shape of her muzzle. She's certainly not a dog!"

Lucie gazed at her in dismay. "But then you haven't helped at all!"

CHAPTER SEVENTEEN
Human Knowledge

Professor Pike stared at Lucie in astonishment. "Whatever is the matter?"

"I *told* you!" Lucie gasped, almost sobbing. "If Fang is a wolf, then they're going to send her away! And you just said she *is*!"

"I said no such thing."

"You did! I heard you!"

"You did not. I said she wasn't a *dog*. But whether she's a wolf...or a weasel...or a wombat, that's another matter entirely!"

"Oh! But she *looks* just like a wolf."

"Only to an untrained eye."

Professor Pike took hold of Lucie's hand.

"Now just you come here a minute, and look, really LOOK. I grant you, at first sight she might look like an ordinary specimen of *canis lupus* — a wolf, in other words. But only to the ignorant observer. Only to somebody who has never really looked at wolves. I have, and I can tell you there are several important differences from any wolf *I* have ever seen."

"Like what?" Lucie asked.

"For one thing, I have never seen a wolf this big. People think that wolves are huge, but actually it's a myth. They are much smaller than people realise. Then there's the eyes. They seem to change colour. Really quite remarkable. The head is even larger than you would expect. This suggests that this animal is highly intelligent — even more intelligent than most wolves, which means very intelligent indeed. Finally, there's her throat and mouth."

Professor Pike peered at Fang's muzzle, apparently not at all worried by coming so close to her teeth. Obligingly, Fang opened her mouth wide to allow the Professor a better look.

"Remarkable," murmured the Professor, almost to herself. "The shape of the mouth. The structure of the throat. *Not* what you would expect at all. Almost....almost as if they are formed to let her *speak.*"

Fang grinned.

"I suppose she *can't* speak can she?" wondered the Professor. And then, before Lucie could reply, "No, no...how ridiculous...ignore that question. I'm afraid I was just getting carried away."

Lucie said nothing.

"So if she *is* a wolf (and it *is* rather hard to see what else she could be) then she is certainly not like any wolf that *I* have seen before," concluded Professor Pike.

Lucie looked from Fang to the Professor and back again. Slowly a smile spread across her face.

"And that would be enough, wouldn't it? That's what you mean. If you were to say that she didn't look like any wolf you had ever seen before...and you *are* an expert after all..."

"Yes," said Professor Pike, smiling. "I think it might be enough."

"And you will tell Mr Dundas what you think? And Mum and Dad?"

"I'll tell anyone you like. The Royal Zoological Society. The International Centre for Canine Studies. The Journal of Animal Anatomy —"

"Mr Dundas and Mum and Dad will do," said Lucie firmly. "Will you come and see them now?"

The Professor shook her head. "No, no. That is not the way. Not for people like head teachers. We can do better than that."

* * *

Wolfie

Outside it was now very dark. In the yellow glow of the streetlights on Acorn Avenue, Alex was playing football with Marcus. He had wanted to play in Marcus's back garden, but Mrs Mainwaring did not allow games: she would not have her lawn churned up into mud, or risk anyone smashing a football into one of her garden ornaments.

Alex tried to slide the ball past Marcus, skidded, and landed in the slush. "Hah!" yelled Marcus, grabbing the ball.

"Let's go in now, Marcus," said Alex wearily. "Mum'll be wondering where I am."

"Call her on your mobile. I just want to show you this great technique I've developed for cutting off the angle —"

Marcus stopped in mid-sentence. Lucie and Fang had just come out of Professor Pike's house. Marcus hurled the football at Alex's face, then ran over to hide behind the gatepost. As Lucie came through the gate he jumped on her.

"Hah!" he yelled.

"Grrr!" said Fang, losing her temper. She snapped at him, as she sometimes snapped at the gulls in the park, only less playfully. Marcus sat down with a thump in the snow.

"Gerr'er off me!" he squawked.

"Don't be silly," said Lucie coldly. "Fang won't bite you."

"Although you deserve it," said Alex, coming up. "Snooping!"

"I wasn't snooping!" Marcus struggled up out of the wet slush. "I was playing football and when I saw Lucie, I — well, I was concerned that she might be bothering Professor Pike. After all, Professor Pike is very — err — elderly."

"Snooping!" said Alex again.

"Anyway what were you doing in there?" Marcus said to Lucie. "What do you want with that old Professor?"

"You don't have to tell him," said Alex.

"I know. But actually I don't mind."

Lucie reached into her coat pocket and drew out an envelope. Very slowly she unfolded it. "Listen:

"To Whom It May Concern

I, Professor Elspeth Pike, Professor Emeritus of Zoology, Fellow of the World Centre of Canid Studies, Winner of the Gold Medal for Contribution to Scientific Understanding given

by the International Distinguished Scientists'
Society, and acknowledged expert on the
species Canis Lupus (Wolves) do hereby certify
that the animal belonging to Lucie Firkettle,
commonly known as "Wolfie", does not meet
those accepted criteria established by
experts in the field and so cannot be
categorised as a member of the Canis Lupus
(Wolf) species.

Yours sincerely

Professor Elspeth Pike, FRS, FSCS, WERE,
Er., Ser, WERWE, Phd.

There was a brief silence.

"What does *that* mean?" demanded Marcus rudely.
"It's gibberish!"

"Don't worry about what it means," said Lucie,
smiling as she folded up the letter. "It's called an
Expert Opinion. And the important thing is —
Professor Pike says it will do the trick!"

"Here, give me that!" And Marcus tried to snatch
the letter. But Alex grabbed his jacket, and Marcus
slipped and fell in the slush for the second time.

"Serves you right!" said Alex.

But Marcus was already up and running for home. It wasn't Alex that had scared him. It was the look he had seen in Fang's eyes. Certified or uncertified wolf, he wasn't going to mess with her!

CHAPTER EIGHTEEN
As It Turned Out

As soon as she got home Lucie showed Professor Pike's letter to her parents. They were both still looking terribly worried and guilty, but as they read the letter all that changed. The worry drained from their faces, the anxious lines on their foreheads vanished and by the time they had finished reading they were almost chuckling.

"Oh well, that's all right then," said Dad. "A wolf indeed!"

"We were crazy!" agreed Mum. "Imbeciles! I mean a wolf — in our house!"

"Professor Pike knows her onions," said Dad. "Or wolves, I should say. If only we'd known she was a World Expert on Canines! We could have sorted this out long ago."

"I'll telephone the vet and cancel that appointment," said Mum, getting up.

The next day Lucie asked her teacher if she could go and see Mr Dundas. As she knocked on his office door, she could see Marcus hanging about at the end of the corridor, near the boys' toilets. *I wonder what he's up to*, thought Lucie. *Still, surely he can't do anything now?*

Mr Dundas was busy chairing an important meeting about school dinners, but he broke off to read Lucie's letter. By the time he had finished reading he was almost smirking. "Excellent, excellent, very good indeed. *This* should satisfy the parents. *And* the governors. *And* the Council. Useful to have a distinguished scientist in the neighbourhood. Maybe I can get her in to talk about her work...."

Lucie listened in astonishment. Somehow a few words on a piece of paper had brought about this great change. Fang was exactly the same animal that she had always been — only now Lucie's parents and Mr Dundas were treating her completely differently. It was as if she had turned from a wolf into a fluffy kitten.

It *felt* like magic. But it was only the power of words.

However, before Lucie could congratulate herself, there was a rap on the door. Without waiting for an answer, Marcus burst in.

"What is the meaning of this?" demanded Mr Dundas.

"I know all about that letter," Marcus began. "But there's something you don't know. Whether that creature is a dog or a wolf doesn't matter. The fact is —" he paused for a moment, looking from face to face — "it TALKS!"

As he finished speaking he shot an especially malicious look at Lucie. *You didn't expect THIS*, it seemed to say. She might have thought she'd wriggled out of her difficulties. But she was wrong. Her biggest secret was out!

There was a brief, charged silence.

Then, "choof-choof-choof" went Mr Dundas. He sounded like an old-fashioned steam train. For a moment Lucie thought he was choking, or having a fit. Then she realised. He was *laughing*.

Lucie began to chuckle too.

Marcus turned crimson. "Aren't you going to tell the police or the zoo or *somebody*!"

"Marcus Mainwaring," said Mr Dundas, when he could speak. "You've given me such a good laugh that I'm going to consider what you said a pure joke. Now get back to your classroom this moment! And no more nonsense!"

And that was the end of that.

It really was. Nobody said anything more about

Fang being a wolf. They forgot all about it. Christmas was coming, and in all the fuss about shopping and presents and carol concerts and parties, nobody was even interested.

"Silver Paw was right," Lucie said to Fang. "*Human knowledge is what you need, Written in form that humans read.* That's what the Expert Opinion was. How did he know?"

"Oh, he's a wise one," said Fang, wisely.

"I wish I could ask him," Lucie said.

One person who did not forget about Fang was Professor Pike. She invited Lucie and Fang round for mince pies, and told them all about her expeditions in the wilderness. They were pleased to learn that although the bones in the glass cases did belong to wolves, they had all died long before Professor Pike had found them.

"I'm too old for any more expeditions," Professor Pike said wistfully. "In fact I never thought I'd see another wolf. But now one turns up on my own doorstep! Something very like a wolf, anyway. Would you mind if I took some photos? I'm thinking of writing an article for the Journal of Canine Studies."

Lucie said she didn't mind at all. And Fang — who was wolfing down her third mince pie — didn't mind either. They both liked the Professor. As long as she did not say where Fang lived — and she had promised she would not — she could write what she liked.

Another good friend, delighted that Fang was safe, was Alex. Although not everything had turned out for the best in his view. For Marcus Mainwaring was now goalkeeper on the school football team. When he had asked Miss Bunting, the school coach, to try out, he had turned out to be so good that she had given him the position on the spot. "Who'd have thought it?" grumbled Alex. "He can't run, he can't dribble, he can't shoot — but he *can* save goals! He's so good we'll never get rid of him!"

"Still, think of all the matches you'll win," said Lucie comfortingly. "And it will take his mind off Fang, and getting her into more trouble."

It was the last day of term. It was snowing again, and Alex and Lucie had met by the gates to exchange presents. Alex had given Lucie a wonderful book about wolves, and Fang a box of Meaty Dog Chews, which she had sniffed then dropped in the snow.

"I'm sure she'll love them," said Lucie quickly, thinking that Fang would much prefer a haunch of venison, and wondering how she could arrange one.

Lucie gave Alex a book about football, and Fang gave him an interesting stick she had found in the woods. Alex said he would put the stick in pride of place next to his football trophies.

Then Fang and Lucie walked home together. The snow was floating down between the branches of the trees. The sky seemed vast, and the houses were dim and dark behind their hedges. Even the cars by the sides of the street looked more like snow-covered igloos.

"What's that?" asked Lucie as an eerie howl echoed through the air. "A wolf!"

"*Wolf?*" exclaimed Fang. "*That* was a cocker spaniel!"

"Oh," said Lucie, blushing.

As they turned into Lucie's garden, she said, "It has been wonderful, Fang, since you came to stay. And now it's Christmas, too. I've never been so happy. There's just one thing. Do you think I'll ever see the other wolves again? Especially Silver Paw? I do hope so!"

Fang smiled her most wolfish smile. "Oh, I think you will," she said. "After all, you are a Wolf Cub of our Pack. Something tells me this will not be the last of our adventures!"

And wolf and girl went inside together.

THE END

Jessica Haggerthwaite: Witch Dispatcher

Emma Barnes

ISBN: 978-1-905537-30-3 (paperback, RRP £6.99)

Also available as an ebook

Jessica has always planned to be a world-famous scientist one day. But her mother has just become a professional witch!

Who will take Jessica seriously now?

To stop her mother wrecking her plans (and breaking up the family), Jessica resolves to show her that no one needs to believe in magic these days. But her plans – like her mother's spells – don't always have the desired effect...

How (Not) To Make Bad Children Good

Emma Barnes

ISBN: 978-1-905537-28-0 (paperback, RRP £6.99)

Ever since she bit Father Christmas when she was six months old, it's been downhill all the way for Martha Bones. She is horrible to her baby brother, Boris, and elder sister, Sally, and her parents are in despair.

Far away, Martha's behaviour comes to the attention of the Interstellar Agency, whose aim is to make bad children good. Fred – who has a poor track record – is sent to Earth as Martha's guardian agent. His mission: to transform Martha into a lovely, likeable child. However, Martha has other ideas!

The King of the Copper Mountains

Paul Biegel

ISBN: 978-1-905537-14-3 (paperback, RRP £5.99)

At the end of his thousand-year reign of the Copper Mountains old King Mansolain is tired and his heart is slowing down. When his attendant, the Hare, consults The Wonder Doctor, he is told he must keep the King engaged in life by telling him a story every night until the Doctor can find a cure.

The search is on for a nightly story more wonderful than the last, and one by one the kingdom's inhabitants arrive with theirs; the ferocious Wolf, the lovesick Donkey, the fire-breathing, three-headed Dragon. Last to arrive is the Dwarf with four ancient books and a prophecy that the King will live for another thousand years – but only if the Wonder Doctor returns in time.